NEXT OF KIN

DEREK JORDAN

<u>Also by Derek Jordan</u>

A Small World

A Small World 2: Seek and Destroy

Drought

Mammon (Coming soon)

Drought 2 (Coming soon)

To: Nicole
Appreciate your
Support!

Derek
J.

3

To God, Nalani, Jaci, Speedy, Anson, friends, the rest of my family, and supporters.

In loving memory of my father, Rudy C. Jordan.

PROLOGUE

January 2014

THE GUSTY WINDS HOWLED in the frigid late morning. The glow from the full moon brightened the bottom half of Walnut Street, and it exposed the few misguided misfits standing in the Arctic weather selling leak to the few zombies that occupied the crime-infested area. At 2:45 in the morning, penniless fiends stopped their campaign for credit and went somewhere with shelter. The two men standing on the porch knocked on the door, and they shivered. Timmy Blairwood knocked for three minutes, but no one responded. Steven Law contorted his face as the bleak weather beat at it. Steve's hands were numb and his round jawline shook as the cold seemed to infiltrate his body. Steve inhaled his Newport and flicked the ashes; he knew something wasn't right. Before Steve and his ace Quincy jacked the kilos he had in the bag, Quincy told him he felt he was being watched and followed. Steven criticized him, but now he felt the same dose of paranoia. It was the third batch of cocaine the men dropped off for Blake to chop up for distribution.

Steven was a short, light-skinned, wiry, bald headed man with no facial hair. His Yankee skully covered the strain on his forehead, and the hunger in his beady eyes. He wore a cheap navy blue winter coat, two mid-sized diamond studs in his ear, wheat hued Timberlands, and black jeans. Steve shoved his negative thoughts to the side and mentally visualized greenbacks, jewels, and a better life for his mother and brother. Steve remembered the dismal days they'd gone through. Steve remembered the ridicule he and his brother endured because of the raggedy clothes they wore to school. Steve remembered how the ridicule pushed him away from school, and away from books while it pulled Steve's younger brother deeper into his books and studies, making him dream of a higher education that Steve could never afford had it not been for the heist. Once Steve and his team flipped the stolen kilos, his brother's education would be chump change, and most importantly, paid in full.

Steve took another pull of his cigarette and exhaled the smoke into the frosty night. Despite his vision, Steve couldn't shake off the thought of something being out of place. The moment seemed eerie to Steve, but he couldn't put a finger on it.

"I'm tryin' to chill, but I can't shake this fucked up feelin' that I'm having. We got life changin' shit in this bag. Blake ain't here to open the fuckin' door, and you calm about this shit," Steven said nervously.

Timmy blew some heat into his hands before he spoke. "You ain't tryin' hard enough. We here early. He may be on his way. Just relax fam," Timmy said as he adjusted the black hoodie on his head. The hoodie and black sweatpants Tim wore were too big for his short sized, frail frame, but just the right size to conceal the Springfield Leatham he kept on him at all times.

Timmy had just come home from prison after doing five years for drug possession. At twenty-seven, Tim spent most of his life locked up in multiple reform schools and penitentiaries. Yellow skinned with a pinch of brown, Tim's eyes were green, and his teeth looked like they belonged to a dog. Tim's life consisted of cruelty to others, murder attempts, warrants, neglect, and rejections.

"Tim, don't test my patience. Fuck do you mean just relax? Do you know how suspect we look right now?"

Tim looked at Steve and displayed his dogged toothed smile.

"We look like two niggas knocking on the door."

A cranberry apple colored Mitsubishi Eclipse approached the two men slowly as they stood on the porch. Steve's paranoia heightened. The driver stopped in front of the three-family home next door and pulled away. Steve and Tim gave one another a puzzled look, and decided to step away from the porch. No one opened the door so it made no sense to linger around with a duffle bag filled with raw. They stepped off the porch and walked through the yard en route to Steve's Buick Regal when a lone figure moved hastily in their direction. When the figure got closer, Steven and Timmy knew the deal. The unknown

NEXT OF KIN

figure wore a black hoodie that concealed his head, and a long black cloth that covered the bottom half of his face. The masked man's eyes spelled murder. When the masked man pulled out his sawed off shotgun, Timmy's street instincts kicked into full gear and he reached for his gun, but he accidentally knocked the tool out of his hoodie. Tim hauled ass as soon as the gun hit the ground. The weight of the duffle bag slowed Steve down as he went for his pistol. It was too late. Steven and the masked man locked eyes. Steve saw death coming upon him as the gunman raised his shotgun, and manually cocked the hammer. The blast was deafening. The impact of the shell tore right through Steve's vital organs and intestines. Blood pooled around Steve as he lay by himself near a gutter. The last person Steve saw before he closed his eyes for good was the masked man who had just taken his life. Steve didn't know that Blake was draped over a chair in the house with a bullet wound in his upper chest.

The killer left Steve's gun exactly where it dropped, and the masked man snatched the Springfield off of the ground that Timmy lost hold of before he collected the duffle bag of leak Steven dropped. The driver of the Eclipse pulled up alongside the gunman and picked him up. The few scattered people around the corner from the area didn't witness the murder, but they heard the shotgun blast and the faint noise of the Eclipse. The driver increased the rpm on the tachometer of the car as the driver made a great escape.

CHAPTER 1

-Six years later

LUKE LAW WAS AWAKENED by the sunlight. It beamed into the bedroom. It was 1:30 in the afternoon. Luke had been sleep since eight in the morning because he worked a double at his group home job. His schedule was three to eleven, second shift. Luke stayed overnight to clock in some hours. He needed the money, as Luke was the only breadwinner of the third-floor apartment. Without the overtime, a bill would be unpaid, or his son Baron would go without a necessity. The mother of his child acted as if she was a trophy because she didn't do or contribute to anything. Luke rose out of his position on the bed, stretched, and wondered what today would bring. He got out of the bed and went straight to the bathroom.

After Luke washed up and shaped his five o'clock stubble, he gazed at himself flatly in the mirror. He was a twenty-five-year-old brown skinned, slim-sized young male that wore a medium sized Afro. His squinty eyes were gentle. His trademark was his chipped front tooth. His normal attire was cheap, faded jeans, cheap sneakers, and faded shirts. He bit his nails constantly. He was calm and laid back, and never had been into any trouble. He was the complete opposite of his older, deceased brother.

Luke walked into the living room and sighed. The third floor two-bedroom apartment was not easy on the eyes. The brown leather couches in the living room sunk inward. Layers of dust coated the ceiling fan. Clothes covered the dirty white, putrid carpet. The kitchen floor had grim and debris from a lack of care. The refrigerator was draped with magnets, menus, and pictures. There were so many dishes piled in the sink that the bottom of it hadn't been seen in days.

1

Baron slept on the soiled carpet near the television in the living room. His diaper was unchanged for a long period of time, and it drooped to the floor. DCF would make a case if they walked through the door. In the midst of the foul odor, filthy and dirty clutter, Talisha laid on the couch and watched Judge Mathis while she toted on a joint. Luke shook his head.

"So this is what it is, huh? You don't work, clean, think, and care for our seed but I'm working doubles everyday to support the household. When I came in from work this morning, I figured you would have this place cleaned by the time I woke up. But no, you want to be Cleopatra and have me work *and* clean. Fuckin' fabulous," Luke said as he picked Baron up, placed him on a clean spot on the couch, and changed him while he slept.

Talisha eyed him coldly, exhaled the smoke, and placed her joint in the ashtray.

"Don't start your shit nigga. I don't have to clean on *your* time. I ain't your fuckin' slave or daughter. You the man of the house and you supposed to care for us. When you say clean, I'm supposed to jump and start scrubbing? Negro please."

Talisha Holloway was misguided. She never had structure or discipline during her childhood. There was no difference in terms of the way she carried herself around her son. Talisha had no skills, will, or desire to compete in the workforce, or to do anything outside of her comfort zone. Talisha was too knee-deep in her second childhood to exert an effort. Her baby soft yellow skin and her small brown eyes were always red when she smoked blunts. Talisha wore an earring in her nose, and her lips were full. Her weave was black, long, and wavy and it was covered with a scarf. She was a mediocre woman with a fucked up attitude toward everyone and everything around her. Talisha was twenty-five, and she was regarded as a "black girl lost." Talisha was born in New Britain, Connecticut, but lived in Waterbury most of her life. She packed on fifty pounds to her former petite physique, and she was self-conscious about it. The swell of her breasts, however, were always display, and Talisha dressed scantily whenever she went out *every* weekend. Talisha was materialistic, and she always wanted shit, but was always broke.

Luke ignored her reply and tended to Baron. Baron was waking up, and he wiped his sleep-crusted eyes on the debris-ridden carpet.

NEXT OF KIN

Luke played with Baron while Talisha nagged him. Luke ignored her bombast. He was too occupied with Baron to give a shit. Luke said what he had to say, and she heard him. That was all that mattered. Luke was too levelheaded to jump out of character and curse her out.

While Luke tickled Baron, his cell phone rang. He knew it was his job calling because of the ringtone. Luke thought something seemed strange; he was due at work for three o'clock. Luke's employer *never* called him an hour-and-a-half before his shift started; he was curious, and Luke answered the call.

"Hello."

"Hi. Luke Law please," the woman's Spanish accent-filled voice stated.

"Yes, this is he."

"Hi Luke, this is Mercedes Rubio from HR. I'm sorry to be calling you at this time, but there has been an incident at your assigned area that requires you to be temporally removed from the company while an investigation is pending..."

"What investigation?" Luke interrupted. He felt Talisha's eyes on him. He took the conversation in the bedroom.

"I'm not at liberty to discuss the matter any further Mr. Law. Someone else will be in touch with you shortly."

"Who will be in touch with me? You're telling me that I am being removed from my post but I don't have the right to know why?" Luke was trying not to shoot down the messenger.

"I'm sorry Mr. Law, but that's policy. We will mail you your check. Remember, this is not a termination. This sort of thing happens all the time. I assure you that you are not alone in this matter. Once again, someone will be in touch with you."

Luke sighed. "Alright."

When Luke got off the phone and opened the bedroom door, Talisha wondered around in the hallway. She overheard the conversation.

"Just fuckin' great. You got fired. You're a real winner. How the hell are we supposed to survive?"

Luke fumed and knew he had to get away from her. Talisha was provocative, but he never landed a finger on her. However, with the way he felt at the moment, he could easily jump out of his zone.

"Real talk Talisha, you need to leave me the fuck alone. I'm not really in any mood for your bullshit."

Talisha smacked her teeth.

"Then you're not in the mood to be paying any bills or caring for our son. What the fuck did you do that was so fucked up that you lost your job over it?"

As Talisha carried on with her bullshit, Luke scrambled around for his toiletries. Luke ignored her as she rambled on. He entered the bathroom while Talisha talked shit. Luke closed the door in the middle of her verbal onslaught. He stepped into the shower and bathed. He could still hear the drone of her voice over the spray of the water, but Luke's mind was on that phone call he just had with HR.

It didn't take him long to get dressed because Luke didn't own a variety of clothes. Luke's attire was typically jeans, t-shirts, sweatshirts, and the same sneakers his mother bought him two years ago. After he put them on, Luke packed Baron's travel bag, and he got him ready for a day with his grandmother. Moments before walking out of the door, Talisha stopped him. They were arm's length away from one another, and she looked at Luke coldly.

"I wish your brother was still alive. We could've borrowed money from him. That nigga never had a job in his short life and still managed to make more than you made in the few years you worked at that low paying, bullshit ass job."

Luke shot deadly daggers at her. The menacing cold look in his eyes and face was something Talisha had never seen. Luke leered at her for twenty seconds, tempted to press her up against the wall, and do damage to his raunchy queen. Despite her belligerence, Talisha backed off because she knew she went too far. Wisely, Luke picked up Baron, and walked out of the apartment. Luke was a second away from leaving a mark on her neck.

After Luke got Baron situated in his car seat, Luke waited a few moments before he started his 2002 Mazda 626. It took a few attempts to start it. He sat still in the driver's seat, reflected on Talisha's harsh words, and banged the steering wheel. He struck it until Baron cried.

NEXT OF KIN

After Luke looked into his son's eyes, he knew he had to be strong for him despite the circumstances.

Luke's cell phone rang. It was Joe, one of his co-workers. Luke put the car back in park, gave Baron a toy he left in the car to keep him occupied, and answered the call.

"What up Luke? I'm pretty sure you got the same fucked up call I got." Joe sounded pissed.

Luke adjusted the phone, and he pulled away from the curb. He drove and talked at the same time.

"Yeah I did. You know what happened?"

"Cindy *just* called me and told me John died last night on *our* shift, and that police think that there is foul play involved."

Luke pulled over to the side of the road abruptly. "Get the fuck out of here! And foul play Joe?"

"That was *my* reaction. Anna found him dead in his bed this morning. Popo thinks that the man was smothered."

"I don't have nothing to do with that shit, but that's fucked up. So now we are guilty until we are proven innocent. Ain't this a bitch? I'm sorry the man lost his life, but I need to get paid," Luke said.

"You and I both. We all do, but I heard it might be a while before the investigation is over. I'm not waiting around. I think I overstayed my welcome there anyway. Time to get another job," Joe said.

"So these cats think we had something to do with that?"

"Yes and no. The company thinks the new consumer did that, but John's family thinks one of us probably did that shit. Just don't be surprised not if, but when the police question you Luke."

Luke gripped the steering wheel. "I swear man, I don't need this kind of shit in my life right now. John's people don't like black people anyway so of course we are the main suspects. Is Herb out of work too?"

"Yup...and Rebecca."

"Damn."

Baron started to cry while Luke and Joe talked. Luke dropped the phone by accident, and Joe continued with the group home death. Luke got back on the phone.

"I'm going to holler at you as soon as I drop my son off at my mother's crib. He actin' up right now." Luke ended the call without giving Joe a chance to respond.

Luke managed to put Baron to sleep. As he drove, he dwelled on what might have happened to John. He checked on him at ten o'clock last night, and he was fine. Something didn't seem right. *Maybe he did that to himself.* Luke contemplated his next move, which was the unemployment office. He wouldn't get paid while he was on administrative leave, and unemployment probably wouldn't pay him that much, but slow money was better than no money.

CHAPTER 2

LUKE SAT AT THE bar in *Victories* slumped over his drink. He felt down on his luck. After he completed his registration with unemployment, Luke decided that going home to Talisha's raucous-filled mouth wouldn't be wise. Instead, Luke called his homeboy Dan Julien to participate in his misery. Luke was having a fucked up day. Luke figured that a drink, a blunt, and a Black and Mild was needed to ease some of the edge of a depressing day that consisted of him being a possible suspect in a patient's death, and listening to Talisha's fucked up choice of words about Luke's deceased brother.

A dark-skinned bartender male served drinks while he, along with the other patrons, watched game 3 of the NBA Eastern Conference Semi-Finals along at the bar. The locals' vulgar language filled the peaceful atmosphere as the basketball junkies of the small crowd placed hundred dollar bets on the game. Everything was cool though. Luke grew up in the neighborhood, and he knew everybody in the small tavern.

Luke was buzzed from the three Jack Daniels and Cokes. Dan was right along with him. He felt the same drunkenness. Dan had his own problems, and Luke's phone call was great timing. Dan known Luke since elementary school, but the two lived on opposite sides of the gate. Dan sold crack, and had his hands in robbery, and a few other criminal attributes. Only twenty-five, Dan done four bids, and currently threw rocks at the prison. Dan had four children, and was prone to engage in beef. Dan was dark-skinned, his hair was always shaved into a bald Caesar, and he kept his facial hair trimmed. Dan's eyebrows were arched like downward slopes, making him look like a villain that never smiled a day in his life. Short and stocky, Dan always spent his drug money on sneakers and denim. Dan was Luke's best friend, but many people on the streets didn't like Dan, and wished him on a coroner's table. Dan was disloyal to many people in his upbringing, but never crossed Luke because of their childhood history, and Luke's position in life. Luke wasn't in the criminal grind, and he was always there when Dan went through fucked up times.

The two men sat somberly at the bar along with everyone else that wanted to keep their stools. The liquor wasn't making anything better. Everyone hollered and screamed while the two men sulked at the bar.

"So Luke, let me get this straight. Your job got you sitting home because a patient died on your shift? All this forensic shit happening and they still can't figure out how the motherfucker died. *Shit,* all them fuckin' meds he swallowed for years caught up to his ass. Y'all gave that dude one Haldol too many."

Luke looked at Dan and smirked. "Fuck you know about Haldol?"

Dan smiled back. "I may be a criminal, but I ain't stupid. Besides, I'm a drug dealer; I sell that shit."

The men shared a brief chuckle.

"And to add more stink to shit, the patient's family ain't so fond of black people."

"How you figure that?" Dan asked.

"Because the family only talk to the white folks that work there," Luke said.

"Ain't that a bitch? And y'all caring for their peoples...or was caring."

"Tell me about it. We did all kinds of shit for that man above and beyond expectations but we never got credit for it. Can you believe his sister thanked Nick, who happens to be white, about his progression and the best day he had all year? Nick told her that it was us to thank, but that bitch never said a word to me or any of the minority staff."

Luke allowed several glasses of liquor to loosen the grip that sobriety normally held on his tongue. He was angry with his employer, and at John's racist family. Luke was out of work, and he leaned on unemployment over some shit he knew nothing about. The man fell asleep at his usual time. Luke checked on him an hour later. The next day, John was dead. Now Luke and his black and Latino co-workers were deprived of making their living. Luke was pissed.

"I feel ya fam. For all they know, another patient could have done that shit," Dan said.

"That's what me and my co-workers said. They blaming the black people before blaming that shit on consumers that have thick and lengthy charts loaded with assaultive behaviors."

The men consumed their drinks, and ordered another round while the occupants chanted for their respective teams.

Dan scrolled through his phone."So what's good with shorty? She still ain't working?"

Luke twisted his face at Dan's question. "The only thing she holding down is a joint and her club passes. That chick hasn't worked since I known her."

Dan shook his head. "If *you* was the one not working, you would've been on your ass fam. She ain't doing shit Luke. Why not kick *her* to the curb. You said it yourself; your child went the whole day without being changed. Luke, you my fam for life and I will always give it to you straight; you are gonna end up doing something real stupid. I know you homie; you pretty reserved and quiet. You a motherfuckin' dormant volcano that's long overdue for an explosion."

Luke looked at Dan and said nothing. Dan was right, and that was what scared Luke. Talisha may have been a bitch in his, Dan, his mother, and many others' sets of eyes, but she was still Baron's mother, and nothing would ever change that.

"It's funny that you mentioned that. Fuckin' Talisha talkin' about if Steve was still alive, we could borrow money from him. And he made more money than I did in my few years of working at my job. Dan, I was seriously going to fuck her up for using my brother's name in that context. I decided to ignore her shitty ass, but that comment caught me off guard."

"I know you was Luke. If I was calm and collect like you, that comment would have easily made me jump out my character, and I end up gettin' locked up."

People cheered and jeered. Luke and Dan loved basketball, but they were unimpressed for the moment. Dan battled trial and tribulation on a daily, consistent basis so his mind was always in the gutter. Luke had his share of problems that consisted of a self-centered woman, a dead consumer at his employer, and lint and candy wrappings in his pockets. Luke was broke, temporally unemployed, and highly stressed.

Dan took a swig of his drink.

"You want some work?"

"I'm good Dan. You know I don't flow like that."

Dan leaned in close to Luke's ear, away from ear hustlers. "I know, but it ain't for your self-interest. It's nature versus nurture homie. Being a true citizen like yourself ain't doing nothing but giving you problems and broke pockets. Besides, you told me you was temporally unemployed. Those unemployment checks ain't coming for at least a few weeks. Or you could tell your woman to hold you down."

Luke placed his hand on his brow and rubbed it. Everything Dan threw at him seemed lucritive, but Luke wasn't built for the game, and he knew it. Dan attempted to introduce Luke to uncharted territory. Steve kept him away from it all. Luke had potential, and the mind to do many things, but his circumstances forbade him to do what he wanted to do. Luke could damn sure use the boost though.

"I'll keep it in mind Dan, but I think this thing is going to be over with soon. I had nothing to do with him dying."

"I hear you talkin' that shit, but if I was in your shoes, I wouldn't take a gamble on my seed. You got to do what you got to do fam. At your spot, you're dealing with a body, not some missing meds. That investigation that's poppin' off at your job could take longer than you think, but on that note, I got to make moves." Dan got up, and he beckoned the bartender over for the tab and tip.

The men dapped one another before Dan headed out the bar. Luke was left alone with his drink and inebriated thoughts. Luke's thoughts centered on Talisha's statement about his brother. He didn't like how Steve's named rolled off her tongue, but in a sense, she was right. If Steve was alive, he would give him a bag of cash, but Steve was long gone.

After he left the bar, Luke started his car, and checked his text messages and phone log. Luke noticed a peculiar phone number along with a few voice messages. After checking them, he chuckled at the detective who left him a voice message. The detective asked Luke to come to the station to answer some questions. He felt like a suspect after that shit. He reached into his ashtray, and relit the Black and Mild. The only thing Luke stressed was his money. The patient's death was an unfortunate incident, but it had nothing to do with Luke.

While in motion, Dan called him, and asked Luke if he could meet him at a bar on Store Avenue. Luke politely declined because he was too drunk, stressed, and overwhelmed with uncertainty to linger around anyone. Luke wanted to go home and think. Understanding his friend well, Dan didn't press him about it, and the men disconnected.

When he drove up Hill Street, a few houses from the neighborhood bodega, Luke's car engine shut down. He wasn't worried because he knew what it was. It was the fuel pump. Luke was thankful that his son wasn't in the car. It was, however, an inconvenience at the moment because he didn't want to be bothered by the hassle. Luke was fucked up off of brown liquor, and he knew he had to muster up the coordination to get his car started.

Luke popped opened the trunk and hood, got out of the car, retrieved the starter fluid from the trunk, and took the neck off of the air cleaner. After he sprayed the starter fluid at the motor, Luke started the car. He closed the hood and trunk, and traveled toward his dwelling near Fleet Street. Luke wanted to get there as soon as possible because what he did to the car was only a temporary fix. It was a fuel delivery problem that needed to be addressed, but Luke needed money to do that.

Luke parked the car in front of the three-family building he lived in. He looked up at the top floor and saw a light on in the bedroom. Talisha was up, and she was the last person he wanted to see. Luke sighed as he anticipated her bullshit. If Talisha weren't the mother of his son, she would had been gone a long time ago. Luke wasn't sure how much more of her bullshit he could take.

Luke pondered his situation for a few minutes before someone that drove a black Lincoln MKX situated the vehicle next to Luke's crasher. Luke rolled down the window to see what the deal was. The driver slowly stepped out of the MKX. The man didn't look familiar to Luke as the stranger made his way to the driver side of Luke's car. The six-foot-five man carried an aura of danger so deep that Luke's intoxication turned to fear. The burly man was bald-headed, and wore a thick beard and mustache. He was at least three hundred pounds of solid flesh. Rocks and gravel crunched beneath his heavy boots. Luke rolled up his window hurriedly and locked the door. The man stepped up to the car, and gazed crazily into it. Luke stared into the eyes of a savage as the big lump of solid mass sized him up. The man produced a sly grin. The man grabbed the gun from his waistband, smashed the window, and yanked Luke through it by his neck. After the man succeeded, the man pulled Luke up to his feet, and hit him with a short and sharp thudding blow that knocked him out. The man picked up Luke's limp body, tied his wrists, legs, and hands together with rope, tossed him in the trunk, and drove away. No one saw a thing.

Luke woke up three-and-a-half hours later bounded tightly to a steel-folding chair. Almost four hours ago, a huge man knocked him out. That was Luke's only recollection. Luke didn't know where he was. He had no memory of the man who tied his limbs together with rope, or the travel time. Luke was dazed and confused. If he had a different personality, Luke would probably scream, but he remained calm despite his circumstances.

Luke sat bounded on a chair in the pit of silence. The light the streetlamp provided was just enough for him to scan his surroundings. Luke saw a few rats run quietly across the debris-infested floor. Remains of small dead animals were scattered all throughout what appeared to be an abandoned warehouse. The big steel pipes took up most of the space on the grimy wooden floor with weeds that grew through the cracks. The entire building was a hardhat area, and very few would go near it. Alley cats, rats, and bats occupied the ramshackle existence.

The faint sounds of crushed glass increased Luke's fear. Luke began to think of any reason why anyone would want to cause him harm. During his panic-stricken frenzy, Luke knew beyond a reasonable doubt that the family of his patient hired the brute to kidnap him. That theory changed once he saw two black men; the shorter one held a Rottweiler on a short leash. Luke recognized the bearded man; he was the one that put Luke in a four-hour coma. The one with the dog wore chunks of ice in both ears. The thick diamond link the other guy wore around his neck probably caused death in South Africa. The diamonds shone like they were supposed to. Luke knew the patient's family was racist so it had to be a mistake, but there was a reason why he was held in restraints.

The shorter man handed the bigger man the short leash that held the dog captive. The short one walked in Luke's direction, stopped in front of Luke, and stared deep into Luke's eyes.

"Greetings. Toby, untie Luke. I'm pretty sure he isn't stupid enough to attempt to escape a couple of guns and a chemically dependent Rottweiler. Let's at least get him comfortable for a brief tour of this dungeon," Ike said smoothly.

Ike Collins, extremely handsome with an evil, warped mind, aimed for murder, and nothing else when it came to money, product, and betrayal. Ike was eccentric, and he wasn't profane. Ike's sideburns resembled knives that pointed at his chin. His tight clothes outlined his slender muscular physique. Ike's eyebrows looked like two thick, black caterpillars, and his mustache was paper-thin. Ike was a medium sized, dark skinned, thirty-eight-year-old man born and raised in Camden, New Jersey, and his hair was cut into a wavy Caesar. Ike spoke with the aura of a professor, and was a fan of Shakespeare and Greek mythology, but was relentless and cruel with no regard for morals and humanity.

Ike was born into a crime-oriented family. Ike's father, Bruno Collins, was locked up at Federal Supermax (ADX) Prison in Florence, Colorado. Bruno caught an eight forty eight charge (continuing criminal enterprise), and sent away for good. Bruno didn't possess an elegant demeanor, and was a tenth-grade dropout, but the love interest Bruno married after his wife died giving birth to Ike did. Elizabeth Romanov-Collins exposed Ike to a swank way of life in the U.S., and many foreign lands while Bruno conducted his illegal dealings inside and outside the country. Elizabeth practically raised Ike, but Bruno introduced Ike to the underworld that consisted of goons, felons, murderers, extortionists, drugs, hitmen, drug dealers, pimps, and death. Ike's father groomed Luke into a heartless and dangerous soul. Ike sacrificed a full scholarship to Yale to grasp a threshold on his father's drug empire, and Ike became the man he was today...a wealthy sociopath.

Ike put many men to sleep, but witnesses tied Ike with one of his heinous murders. After nineteen years of dope enterprise, extortion, and murder, Ike was arrested for murder, and held without bail despite his stretched-out money. One of the witnesses was ambushed off the road, and killed when the car exploded after it fell five thousand feet onto a stretch of highway. The other witness was mildly retarded (his attorney's discovery through school records), and the statement the witness provided wasn't credible, and it was conflicting. The third witness recanted their original statement because of multiple threats. The trial was dismissed after the other witnesses recanted their statements out of fear. There was no proof, but everyone involved in the short-lived trial knew the witness's death wasn't an accident. Ike's trial ended with an acquittal. After being set free, Ike sought revenge against those who crossed him while he was locked up, which included the kin of the incarcerated and deceased that bailed out of the earth or society without Ike being paid the money or product that was owed to him. Anyone who didn't know Ike would think he was a pussy because of his intelligent dialect, but the unfortunate ones who tried Ike paid the price with their life.

"Sure thing boss," Toby replied obediently.

Luke was horrified. Every one of his muscles went rigid. Luke's body was petrified stone. Luke still couldn't understand why the man knew his name, and why the guy had any interest. Luke never crossed anyone. Luke knew his ordeal wasn't Steve related because he was long buried and gone.

When Toby stood him up, Ike put his hands up, and Luke flinched.

"No need to be startled Luke. Toby wasn't supposed to harm you, but to lead you by gunpoint, not force, and I promise you; he will be dealt with accordingly." Ike looked at Toby coldly. Toby lowered his eyes submissively.

Luke began to relax a little, but he was sober and on full alert. Luke wanted to get out of there, and into a safe haven. Luke looked into Ike's eyes and saw evil. Ike smelled fear, and smiled at the scent of it as he watched Toby free Luke from his restraint. Luke was a little relaxed, but his nerves betrayed him. Luke's heart pumped blood and fear as the henchmen started the one room tour.

"You're probably wondering why you're held captive, correct?" Ike asked.

Luke nodded his head.

"I want to ensure you that you are the right person Toby was told to track down, and I have not mistaken you for your late brother Steven. My condolences by the way."

Luke looked at Ike strangely as the two men assisted him through the dilapidated warehouse.

"However, your brother is the focal point of the matter." Ike pursed his lips after the statement, and continued to pace with his hands crossed behind the small of his back.

"How is that?" Luke asked, the first words he said since the duo's arrival. Luke was certain now that the men were the ones that murdered Steve, or knew who was responsible. Luke was too fearful to produce any anger because he wasn't sure if he would leave the warehouse alive.

"We had nothing to do with your brother's murder," Ike said as if he read Luke's thoughts and continued. "But I did see him a little before his expiration."

"Do you know who..."

"Very predictable Luke," Ike said, cutting him off. "Even if I knew who killed your sibling, that information would come with a hefty price. You would spend years working at your residential place of employment to gather up that kind of coin. But for the record, no, I don't know who killed him."

"Why am I down here then?"

"Again, very predictable, but an acceptable question. Because you are his next of kin. Your brother robbed me out of an entire supply, plain and simple Luke. I want from you *everything* Steve took with him when he left my property, which is approximately one point five million."

A silence crept upon them. Luke looked for any sign on Ike's face that spelled a joke, but Ike's face remained grim and serious. Luke barely cracked twenty-nine thousand a year, and the man demanded Luke to come up with one point five million. Luke wanted to take a shit.

"Sir..."

"Ike. You just made me feel like I was *before* my cohort group." Ike chuckled.

Luke wiped his clammy hands on his clothing to rid them of sweat. "With all due respect, I'm a working man that provides for my family. How am I supposed to come up with a few mill'? Whatever business you and Steve had in the past, I was unfamiliar with it."

While Luke rambled, Toby abruptly yanked Luke to a standstill at the back corner of the warehouse. They rested upon an old, weathered desk behind the extinct assembly line. With little visibility in that area of the warehouse, Luke was able to make out three amorphous shapes posted against the wall. Ike seemed as if he pondered something.

"I'm sad to say this to you Luke, but we all live in an unfair world. It is my utmost displeasure and total disdain to introduce you to three people who were out compliance with reality. That reality is right before your eyes."

Confusion masked Luke's face.

"What reality?"

A sinister grin formed on Ike's face.

"This reality."

On cue, Toby flashed the LED flashlight at the shapes. Luke gasped. Three foul-smelling bodies, all decomposed African American men, were aligned against the wall, dressed in bubble coats, sneakers and denim that faded in the dangerous climate of the warehouse. The bodies were wide mouth-mouth, and chewed up by rats. Dental records would be needed to reveal the names of the bodies. Luke was stunned and continued to gaze at the bodies. Luke's relaxation withered, and his fear bloomed. Ike wore a flat look on his face. He loved the smell and sight of fear. Luke put all the signs on full display. After Luke leered at the bodies, he vomited. Luke never saw a body in a position where it dropped. Luke's vomit agitated the Rottweiler, and the dog barked.

Ike gripped his dog's leash tight. "Enough!"

The dog whimpered, cried, and sat.

While Ike entertained himself with Luke's fear, he dug in the inside pocket of his leather jacket, and pulled out some pictures. Ike beckoned Toby to grab a chair for their guest. As soon as Luke sat, Ike went behind him, and patted him on the shoulder before he dumped the pictures of his family on his lap.

NEXT OF KIN

"I'm pretty confident that you don't want to see Baron or Renee like that now would you?"

Luke wanted someone to wake him up out of his nightmare badly, but the reality of the ordeal was an unfortunate one. Ike knew about Luke and his family. The only way Ike had access to Luke's family was through Steve, but Luke knew Steve wouldn't go that route, or would he? Luke was a millisecond away from an involuntary bowel movement. He was petrified. Luke shook his head. He didn't want to see his only offspring and his mother dead because of a six-year-old debt.

Ike casually stepped in front of Luke, towered over him, bent slightly, and whispered into Luke's ear.

Ike pointed at the seated cadavers. "Get my money, or I'll exterminate your whole family. Tell the police about me, and you'll join these peasants."

"And if you're thinking how I know your whereabouts, job, family, travels, and everything else I didn't tell you about, I am powerful. I could have your whole circle shot dead in a nanosecond. Now be a dear and remove yourself from my premises." Ike turned to face his inferior.

"Toby."

"Yeah Ike."

"Escort Mr. Luke Law to the nearest train station, and make sure he gets there and on the train safely. I need him unharmed so he can perform his task effectively. If what I just said fell on your deaf ear, I'll cut it off. Now am I clear on this?"

"Yeah," Toby said.

Toby didn't like the threat, but the money he made under Ike outweighed all of his extra bullshit. Toby forcefully pulled Luke to his feet, turned him around, tied him with the same restraints he tied him up in earlier, and pushed him a little, slighted about being threatened. Ike paid him no mind, and he tended to his dog.

After being untied in the car, Luke went into the tight bathroom on the train, and he shitted for five minutes. The stench became noticeable to all, but Luke didn't give a fuck. The only thing on Luke's mind was death, and how it had the potential to come his way, even his family. Luke's mind scrambled for answers. He'd just been forced into a world of shit. Luke was literally forced into Steve's debt.

After he used the compact train bathroom, Luke walked out of it, and was greeted by a sea of faces. Luke meticulously walked through the aisle. He knew he was funky. Luke's armpits stank, *and* he just took a liquid shit. Luke was so fucked up from the tragic events that his self-consciousness was tossed out the window. Luke saw an open seat next to an elderly man who had his head against the window, and the old man slept with his mouth open. Luke seized the opportunity and sat. He recalled the events of the early morning. Luke only remembered he left the club by himself, woke up bounded to a chair, and given a brutal ultimatum. Luke found out he was in New Jersey when Toby ditched him at the train station. He had a lot of shit to figure out. Rampant thoughts of Baron and his mother settled in his mind like a plaque. Luke's racing thoughts lowered his eyelids until he reached Connecticut.

CHAPTER 3

LUKE WALKED INTO THE fusty apartment with a deep, dark fear scribed on his face. After waking up on the train when it landed in Waterbury, his hangover blended into his newfound fear. Luke's head ached. His entire body reeked of alcohol, funk, cigarettes, weed, Black and Milds, and death. Luke felt numb, and he was drenched with uncertainty. The walk from the train station was uneventful because it was long, but the fresh air provided Luke a little justice.

Talisha lay around the house with her stomach hanging out as usual while she smoked a blunt near the half opened window. She held a Poland Spring water bottle loaded with phlegm. The television displayed a Lincoln Tech commercial that was suited for the unemployed. The apartment was in total chaos, but Luke's mind was extended above that. Images of three dead bodies paraded through his mind. Luke's mouth was ajar, and his eyes were glassy. Luke was traumatized about being kidnapped, and exposed to folks that would never have a proper home going.

Talisha died out her weed and gave Luke an uncongenial leer. She looked right past the war etched out in his face. Luke's lip was severely bruised, and a mouse-sized knot decorated his closed eye. Talisha was clueless about what her man just went through. She didn't care. Talisha just wanted to know why Luke didn't come home last night or in the morning, but in the late afternoon. It wasn't as if Talisha gave a couple of fucks; she was stuck with Baron.

"Triflin' ass nigga," Talisha said. "Where the *fuck* was you last night? Don't even got the decency to call or radio a bitch. I tell you one thing Luke, don't say shit when I do it. I had plans last night, and you sabotaged my shit. And what bitch you had your dick in for your face to look like that? Look at you; you look like shit, and you fuckin' stink."

Luke ignored her boisterous insults. Talisha rambled on while Luke picked the baby up. Her annoying voice didn't wake Baron, but he felt the hands of his dad, and it made him smile in his sleep. Talisha's mouth moved a mile a second while Luke carried Baron into the bedroom. After he got Baron settled into his crib, Luke viciously slammed the door in Talisha's face. When Talisha finally closed her mouth, Luke mustered up enough strength to gather all of her provocative clothing, toiletries, and shoes and toss them into the hallway.

The decayed faces of the corpses Luke encountered last night woke Luke out of his sleep. Luke's sleep was so deep that he didn't hear Baron cries of hunger from his crib. Talisha was long gone from the apartment, and she hadn't fed him before she left. Luke slowly rose from his position in the bed, and he took Baron out of his crib. After he changed, washed, and got Baron settled, Luke fed him. Tears pooled in Luke's eyes, and they began to spill down his cheeks as Luke stared into the eyes of his only offspring. Luke vowed that he wouldn't let anyone or anything harm his son. Luke had to be strong for Baron. Sitting around being traumatized wasn't going to save his family. Luke had to give into the dark decision he dreaded most; he had to play Ike's game. Luke had to pay Steve's debt. An unspoken confidence overcame him. Luke never sold a drug in his life, but he knew it was either "all in" or "fold." Baron found a comfort spot on his dad's chest and cuddled. Luke put his arm around him, and contemplated his next move.

Baron slept in his car seat while Luke searched the streets for Dan. All of his messages went straight to Dan's voicemail. Luke hoped and prayed that he didn't get locked up when he needed Dan the most. Last night, the proposition Dan offered Luke seemed far-fetched because the drug game wasn't in his nature. Today, things were dramatically different. Luke needed to operate on a capo status. Nickel and dime bullshit wasn't going to keep Luke and his family alive.

Luke rode slowly on North Main and East Farm Street. When he drove at the top of East Farm, Luke dialed Dan's number again.

Luckily, Dan turned on his cell phone because it rung. Dan picked it up on the sixth ring.

"What's good fam? Been tryin' to holla at you all day. Everything straight?" Dan asked.

Luke pulled over abruptly. He got the attention of a few onlookers, but continued their travel.

"No, not at all. I have to see you yesterday. This shit is crazy. I have to see you face to face. I don't give a fuck what you're doing, real talk. Shit is *beyond* insane fam. I'm in a pile of shit right now," Luke said evenly.

Dan sensed the urgency in Luke's voice. Luke was a standard, law-abiding, tax-paying citizen who had never been in any form of trouble. Dan *knew* something was up. He hoped he didn't strangle Talisha.

"I just walked out of the bar. On the corner now."

"I'll be there in thirty seconds."

"So let me get this straight; you're telling me that this big ass nigga knocked you out, kidnapped you, and you woke up in Jersey, and a nigga named Ike gave you an ultimatum? And this is about Steve? *And* these niggas showed you bodies to intimidate you?"

The contorted look on Luke's slightly battered face spelled pain and fear mixed with uncertainty. Luke looked around, especially over his shoulder. Fidgety and horror stricken, Dan read all of Luke's cues as Luke explained his sudden, abrupt disappearance last night. What Luke told Dan seemed far-fetched, but Dan knew better. Dan never seen his friend in a fearful state of mind. Luke's hands shook as he replayed last night's events. When Luke concluded the story, a local cat tapped on Luke's back window, and it startled the fuck out of Luke. Luke flinched and placed his arms over his head instinctively. Dan, on the other hand, pulled out his Ruger, and he leered at the motherfucker through his hostile eyes. It was one of Luke's friends; the short, stumpy man banged on the glass out of fun, but Luke's friend did that shit at the wrong time. Dan stepped out of the car, approached the dude, and pistol-whipped him. The guy fell against the hood of Luke's car in a daze.

"What the *fuck* is wrong wit' you? I should blow your fuckin' face off!"

The incident drew a small crowd. Luke thought the incident brought too much attention, but he kept quiet. Despite the loud noise, it didn't wake Baron. One of Dan's people calmed him. Dan removed his gun from the man's temple, and for the hell of it, he shoved the man to the ground and spat on him. Dan got back into the car with the gun in his hand.

Dan believed everything Luke told him. Dan wasn't surprised by anything, especially if Luke's ordeal was Steve related. Luke's battered face provided a stunning reality. The men sat in the middle of the hood with a child in the car amongst the wolves that sleep during the day, and roam and prowl at night. Luke gave more information on Ike's character before Dan chuckled.

"Real talk Dan. You would think this dude was in an Ivy school, but the motherfucker is more evil than Satan."

"Word?" Dan asked.

"Word."

"Luke, you know I'm gonna ride with you, but just understand that niggas may bleed and die. Your back is against the wall now fam. This nigga told you to give him one point five mill' or end up like the bodies he clipped. It's like a sword fight where no one backs down. You either win or die. You either get one point five million or get killed. It ain't gon' be got by sittin' in this bucket being shook."

"I know," Luke said, looking again over his shoulder.

"You sure you never seen this cat before? You never heard of him or anything?"

"Dan, I wish I knew who the fuck he is, but I don't. I've never seen the dude, and I don't forget a face."

The men sat in stone silence. They tried to make sense of everything. Luke continued to watch his back. Dan pondered thought after thought, and he wondered if someone Steve knew leaked the robbery and Luke's profile. How else would Ike know about Luke's life? Either way, Dan was down to ride with Luke. Dan could recall all the times Luke was there to keep his head above water. Helping Luke, however, wasn't the problem. The problem was the question of whom. Luke could make out Ike's physical description and the dude that knocked him out, but not the invisible men. Dan was ready to go to war for Luke, but Dan had no idea on who he was up against. While Luke continued his trance of the ordeal, Dan unconsciously looked out the window and saw Talisha and her friend being surrounded by four thirsty, bum, broke men. Dan and Talisha locked eyes before she broke her gaze, but Dan continued to mean mug her. Dan secretly wished that Talisha was the bad news, but bad things happen to good people. Luke was in a fucked up predicament. Taking note of Luke's oblivion, Dan had to check him.

"Get out of that trance shit. Niggas get killed being distracted by their own fear. Embrace it fam. This dude Ike ain't immortal; he bleed and shit just like we do. The only thing that bothers me is that invisible men shit. Motherfuckers probably know we having this conversation. Let's go get another crasher. We have to drop off your seed. Your mom home?"

Luke nodded. Dan pulled the gun out of his waistband, wiped it clean, and handed it to Luke. Luke held the gun as if he held the Holy Grail.

"Yeah fam, your hands is a little dirty now. Now you have to get them filthy. This ain't your attribute in life, but right now, it is."

CHAPTER 4

RENEE LAW'S RAISED RANCH home on Columbia Blvd was built a few years before Steven was born. The lawn and shrubs were freshly manicured. The vegetable garden took up a portion of the half-acre of property. An old basketball rim sat crookedly on top of the one car garage. A long, silver fence surrounded the house. With each season that passed, Renee decorated the house to suit each particular holiday. The home was cozy, and it had looked the same since her husband bought it. When Renee's husband died unexpectedly twenty years ago, Renee used some of the money her husband left behind and paid for the house in full.

The house was immaculate. Area rugs flanked the wooden floor. A huge grandfather clock that chimed every half hour stood in the small foyer. Framed pictures of relatives covered an entire wall in the living room. Pictures of Steven, Luke, and their deceased dad covered the majority of the other wall. Many of the other pictures of Luke and Steven were from the heyday of their childhood and adolescence.

After Luke and Dan entered the dark house and took their shoes off, Dan sat on the couch. Luke walked to his mother's bedroom with Baron asleep in his arms. Wil, a guy Renee had dated for six months, lay on top of the bed. He wore only a pair of black striped boxers, and he slept soundly. Luke placed Baron in the crib in the bedroom. Luke walked out of the room, and he looked at Dan incredulously and threw his arms up. Dan cracked a smile, but didn't understand the hatred Luke had towards his mother's arrangement; however, there was nothing Luke could do or say about it. Wil had never given Luke any reason for him to feel that way. Luke would admit that he was a tad jealous of Wil, but Luke knew his mother was vulnerable because of the death of Steven, and Luke didn't want any man to take advantage of her.

Luke knew where his mother was. He was so distraught that Luke forgot his face was fucked up; the last thing he wanted to do was worry his mother. When Luke approached Steven's old bedroom, he found Renee sitting on the bed. She cried and whimpered, and she clutched a framed photo of Steven to her bosom. After six years, Luke knew she would never get over Steven's death. Renee held the framed photo for dear life, and she rocked back and forth with it. Luke cringed at the timing, but he needed a boost. Luke needed some fast cash.

"Ma."

Renee put the picture down on the bed next to her, and she wet the back of her hand with her tears. Renee, forty-seven and brown skinned, was a spitting image of both of her children. Renee was stern, and she made her living as a receptionist in a doctor's office. She'd been there for twenty years. Renee tried to raise her children as best as she could, but the streets took Steve with a strong, solid vice grip. Luckily, Luke spared Renee a lot of heartache throughout the years. Ever since the death of Steven, Renee hadn't been right. All of her emotions that surrounded Steve's death were repressed. Renee worked excessively and cleaned the house, car, and her office constantly. She wore a mask of peace and love, but underneath it was anger and depression. Luke knew about her repressed emotions, but whoever was on the outside that looked in didn't know any better. Many thought Renee handled her eldest son's death well; a few thought she didn't care, but Luke knew better. That wasn't the only time he witnessed her episodes of grief. Luke wished she wasn't in the middle of one of them on this night. Ordinarily, Luke would rather struggle than to ask his mother for money, but he needed the cash, and he needed it now. Since the light was dim, there was a *slight* chance she wouldn't see the war on his face.

"Where's my grandbaby?" Renee asked. She placed the photo back on the dresser, and wiped her eyes and nose. Luke turned away from her so she wouldn't get a visual of his bruised and battered face. Unexpectedly, Renee flicked on the main light, and she caught a glimpse of his face.

Renee's eyes grew wide. "Luke, what happened to you?"

"Ma, no need for you to worry at all. It was a simple misunderstanding. I was leaving the apartment when three dudes jumped on me. When they took a good look at me when I was down, they realized their mistake, apologized, and left."

Renee gently grabbed each side of his jaw, and moved Luke's head as she examined the damage.

"That's why I wasn't comfortable with you moving in with that fast ass baby mother of yours. It ain't nothing but trouble down there where you live," Renee said.

"It's not even like that. You act like you ain't from the hood." Luke stepped away from her examination. Luke walked to the kitchen with Renee in tow.

"Don't get smart Luke, and for your information, I'm far from being ashamed of being from the ghetto, but when you walk in here looking like God knows what, it worries me to death that I buried one child, and the other one gets randomly attacked. You could've been killed!"

"Can you keep it down Ma? Dan is in the living room."

Dan heard every word being exchanged between Luke and his mother, but Luke didn't care if Dan heard them or not. Luke used Dan as a tool to avoid being lectured. Dan was like family, and he received his fair share of lectures from Renee as well. Lecture meant time, and time wasn't on Luke's side. He wasn't fond of his mother's arrangement with Wil, but was thankful he stepped into the kitchen. That meant no lecture. Wil said hello, but Luke only nodded in return. Renee was ready to put Luke's rudeness on blast until Dan walked into the kitchen.

"Hello Renee." Dan through his street demeanor out the window. He walked to Wil and introduced himself. Dan called Renee by her first name because she treated him like the third brother to Renee's two children. Dan remembered their high school years when he had no money for school clothes. Renee provided for him. She took him shopping along with Luke and Steven. Even if Mary, Dan's mother, had the money for his school clothes, she'd smoke it. Renee had known Mary since high school, and could recall her golden years of innocence, but the streets took over Dan's mother and enslaved her. Dan was always hungry, and Renee always fed him. She didn't agree with Dan's current lifestyle, but Renee never judged him.

Dan and Renee hugged. "Hi Daniel. How are you?"

"I'm good. Trying to stay out of trouble. And yourself?"

"I'm doing, but apparently, Luke doesn't know how to stay out of trouble. His face is a mess, and he has a bona fide bum sitting at home doing absolutely nothing. It makes me sick."

Luke looked at his mother like she revealed a secret. "Ma!"

"Don't Ma me. Daniel knows the truth. The only good she ever did in her life was bringing my grandbaby into the world, and that's it."

Dan couldn't help himself. He put his head down, and he laughed. Wil remained neutral.

Luke ignored Dan's laughter, and he walked by Will without acknowledgment. "Ma, I got more pressing matters at hand. I have to talk to you in private."

Luke and Renee walked into the guest room in the back of he house, and Luke closed the door.

While Dan and Wil shared a quick chat, Renee became livid when Luke asked for five thousand dollars. She was hysterical about Luke's removal from his job because of a patient's death. Luke's battered face, temporary removal from his job, the severity of the reasoning, and his request of five thousand dollars didn't sit well with her. Luke said he was backed up on the rent. Renee blasted him about Talisha being a non-factor in the household, and how worthless she was. Luke felt like shit for lying to his mother like that, but he felt he did it for Renee's best interest, which was true. Renee was only a receptionist, but she saved a lot of the money Luke and Steve's father left them. Luke knew she had it. Since Luke had no choice *but* to make money, and a load of it, it wouldn't be a problem to pay it back to her. If Luke paid Renee back quickly, Renee would get suspicious, and it would be something new to worry about.

"I need to think about it Luke, and I'm not making you any promises."

Luke took a deep breath, and exhaled a bit out of inpatience. If Renee wasn't Luke's mother, Luke would add more urgency in his tone, but he knew he had to be careful with her because she would be suspicious. Luke needed the money now. He needed cash money. If

Renee understood the truth, and the magnitude of his circumstance, she wouldn't have Luke wait. If Renee wrote him a personal check, it could take a few days to a week for it to clear.

"Ma, this is serious. The landlord is ready to evict us."

Renee put her hands on her hips and raised her eyebrows. "Now how is that my problem? That woman in your apartment needs to get off her ass and contribute. She is so *sorry*!"

"Can we take a ride to the bank in the morning?" Luke ignored his mother's belligerence.

Renee looked at him strangely. She took in Luke's cuts and bruises again, and matched that with his urgent need of five thousand dollars.

"You're not into any kind of trouble, are you? What's going on Luke? And don't lie to me."

The look Renee wore on her face revealed fear. Her first instinct told her Luke was in trouble. There was more to what Luke was telling her. The look on Luke's face spelled deception.

"I'm just trying to keep a roof over my head, and be on point with the bills. So can we go to the bank in the morning and grab that; will you have it? This landlord has been on my ass about this rent."

"And Talisha just laid up. She's doing nothing but getting fat off of your hard work."

"Ok Ma, that's enough Talisha bashing. She is a lot of bad things, but she is Baron's mother."

"Don't give me that Baron's mother shit Luke. There is a grown woman in your apartment that you share a child with. You're behind on rent, she doesn't have two nickels to rub together, and you're coming here asking for money. Don't *ever* tell me not to Talisha bash. Her triflin' ass needs to be giving *you* money, not me."

Renee was right, and there was no argument. As the silence grew thicker, Luke avoided eye contact with his mother. He didn't mean to be pushy, but lives were at stake. Luke never got any wins with her so he decided to be patient.

"Alright Ma, but the sooner the better. Landlord keeps threatening to evict us."

After he kissed Baron while he slept, Luke followed his mother into the living room where Dan and Wil waited. After Luke and Dan walked out the door, Renee embarked on a new stream of worry and anxiety. When Wil went back to sleep, Renee sat on the sofa and continued to gaze outside her living room window. Luke's visit and request for five thousand dollars startled her. Renee knew Luke was lying about something. The wounds on his face betrayed him.

After the men left Renee's house, Luke sulked, and he stared into space out of the passenger window. Dan drove and texted at the same time, and he bopped his head to "Chopper in the Car," by Rick Ross and Lil Wayne. Once Dan was done texting, he put his phone in the cup holder, turned the music up, and headed to the highway.

"Wil seem like he's cool; pretty down to earth if you ask me. He may have good intentions for your mother."

Luke took himself out of his stupor.

"He may, but I don't know Dan. You know I walked in on my mother holding on to Steve's picture."

The expression on Dan's face didn't change.

"She lost a child fam. She may never get over that, especially the way he was killed."

"That's why I feel a certain kind of way about Wil. I don't want this dude taking advantage of my mom's state of mind. She ain't right and you know it Dan."

"I hear you, but you know as well as I do that Steve wouldn't want your mom or you to lay y'all heads in pity."

Dan and Luke drove all the way across town, engrossed in a conversation about Renee. When Dan drove on the highway, I-84 Westbound, Luke's curiosity peeked.

"Where we going?"

Dan etched a sinister smile.

"Southbury."

"Southbury? For what?"

"To take the first plan of action. You have to stay in the car though, but I'll only be a minute. This lic might be a lot easier than I thought," Dan said as he coasted up the highway.

CHAPTER 5

LUKE SAT AT THE kitchen table in silence. The bruises on his face had subsided a bit, but it was still noticeable. A week went by since Luke received the impossible ultimatum from Ike to repay Steve's debt. The trauma of the ordeal in New Jersey continued to hurt him. Baron was still over his mother's house. Lingering thoughts of Ike, Toby, the bodies, and the task forced upon him were the only vibrations in his mind that echoed loudly. Luke knew he had to toughen up. Being preoccupied with what happened to him would land him in a plot in a cemetery. Luke allowed some of the fear he possessed to gradually drain from his body as his mind recalled a story he once read. It was about a great warrior who was forced to make a crucial decision that would guarantee his survival. The warrior decided to command his men to burn all the ships that brought them to the stage for their battle. That way, his men would have no transportation off the island. It was either survive or succumb to their enemy. The great warrior's men won the battle with that concept in mind. Luke started to mentally embrace the warrior's philosophy, but still lacked the internal motivation to follow his path to courage.

Talisha destroyed Luke's next thought as she walked into the kitchen. She wore a white tank top, and a pair of thong-underwear. Her stomach protruded slightly over the band of her panties, but the tank top straps were too thin to cover her silver dollar sized areolas. Talisha walked seductively in his direction. Luke felt his manhood thicken as she embraced him. Talisha massaged the back of his head, pulled his head into her large chest, and kept Luke's head there. Luke sucked her nipple softly as her tit fell out of the tank top. Talisha worked herself off him, but stayed between his knees. She took Luke in her mouth and performed a deep stroke, and she left a trail of saliva on his dick. While still on her knees, Talisha took one free hand and massaged her clitoris. She stroked herself as she moaned and writhed with pleasure, while she simultaneously stimulated herself and Luke's cock. Unable to tolerate any more foreplay, they took their sensual duties to the bedroom. They didn't bother to remove the clutter of laundry piled on top of the bed.

After Luke mounted Talisha, he couldn't help but notice the lack of walls in Talisha's treasure chest. Luke grabbed her by her love handles, and he started to pump rapidly while Talisha met his every stroke. Suddenly, visuals of the bodies from Ike's warehouse invaded his mind. Luke tried not to lose his erection. The more he sexed her, the more Luke began to believe she was fucking someone else. Talisha became an instant turn off. No matter how much he tried, Luke couldn't get his dick to stay fully erect. He thought about all the late nights, disrespect, tension, the tension Talisha had with his mother, the mystery behind Talisha and her mother's falling out, and most importantly, the lack of care she provided for Baron. Talisha's overall character disgusted Luke. She yelled and moaned loudly with Luke's limp dick inside of her, but he knew she was full of shit. Luke's penis started to get hard when he thought of her friend Melanie. He got his momentum back. Luke gave her seven long deep strokes before he pulled out, and exploded on her buttocks. Talisha rose from the bed with a sullen look on her face. She glowered with disappointment about Luke's poor performance as she made her way to the bathroom, but she begrudgingly understood his difficulty. Talisha remembered the times when Luke could hardly keep his hands off of her. Today, Luke's dick went soft while hedipped into her walls of pleasure. Talisha gained weight, and she always gave Luke hell. Talisha's friend Melanie would bash her for the way she treated Luke. While Talisha loved him because he was the father of her only child, she wasn't in love with him. Talisha speculated that Luke could feel the vibe. When Talisha came back to the bedroom, Luke was asleep. After she rolled a blunt, she stepped out for a few hours. Baron was still over at Renee's house, and she had nothing but time on her hands.

Luke rose at seven in the morning. Talisha was at his side, and she still wore the same clothing from last night. She'd been out, but had somehow managed to make it back to bed before Luke opened his eyes. Luke could smell the stench of alcohol on her as she snored. He glared at her long and hard and realized that, despite any child's need for their mother, he had to cut her off. Talisha didn't have on her trademark thongs. The smell coming from her vagina was a dead giveaway, but the dried semen on her leg was the one-two punch that blew Luke away. Talisha's sleep was induced by her Ciroc intake. Luke placed his nose closer to her pussy for better confirmation and got it; it smelled like a used condom in conjunction with sweaty sex.

After taking a sniff of her vagina, her phone vibrated on the wooden floor from a text message. Talisha didn't budge from the noise of it. Since she was out cold, curiosity drove Luke to invade her privacy. Since Talisha had an ancient T-Mobile flip phone, it wasn't difficult for Luke to check and scroll through her messages. Many of the text messages were from Melanie, but the unopened text message that came from an unknown caller heightened Luke's suspicion. When he clicked it, it read: *This is your mistress sweetness. I hope you realize you left your thong over here. You slipping Tee. Anyway, hit me up if you want me and my man to pound dat ass again (smiley face).* Luke looked at her long and hard. He tried to maintain his strong composure. A strong urge overcame him to shake her out of her sleep, but instead of waking her up, he smiled grimly at her and shook his head. Luke would pretend he didn't know, and to keep his foot on her neck if Talisha ever hit an intense downward spiral in her life.

CHAPTER 6

LUKE WAS COMING OFF a solid high as he pulled onto Union Street. He needed to kill a little time before he partook in the lic he heard from Dan over breakfast and a blunt. Since it was still relatively early, Luke figured the best way to ease his anxiousness and fear was to get lost in a good book. Luke regretted that he smoked that piff with Dan. It increased his paranoia tenfold, and Luke felt stuck. After he parked and turned the car off, Luke pulled Visine out of his pocket and inserted a few drops into each eye. Luke's eyes were red, and their clarity needed to be replenished.

The classical music oozed out of the store speakers when Luke entered *Barnes and Noble*. The music began to sooth his mind. Luke's rampant thoughts were littered with images of decomposing bodies. The music provided him a little therapy. Luke walked through isles and around people who sat with their legs crossed, and he headed towards the self-help section.

After he thumbed through a few books, Luke landed on *Think and Grow Rich* by Napoleon Hill. Satisfied with his selection, he headed towards the front of the store to grab a seat. Luke bypassed a seated businessman that typed ferociously on his laptop before taking a seat. Fifteen minutes into his book selection, Luke traded glances with a Spanish woman, but didn't pay it any mind until he caught her glance again. Instead of taking her possible interest as a compliment, Luke placed his defensive guard as high as he could. The woman *could* be one of Ike's cronies, Luke thought, as he read the last paragraph of the second chapter, and eased his eyes in the woman's direction again. She took occasional glances at him, and Luke caught onto a few more of them. Luke lost all hope that she was interested in him when he realized his face was fucked up, and it was probably the biggest distraction in the store.

Luke began to read another chapter. The attractive woman wasn't in his line of vision. Luke's paranoia dissolved a little, but he wasn't ready to toss caution to the wind. About twenty minutes later, Luke was in the history section. He browsed *Battle Cry of Freedom: The Civil War Era* by James M. McPherson, a book Luke was near completion with. He read books in the bookstore because Luke couldn't afford to buy any. When Luke took his face out of the book, he saw the Spanish woman again, but this time, she browsed through the books while she held *The Lost Symbol* by Dan Brown. Luke grilled the side of her flawless face. When he saw her a few minutes ago, Luke didn't realize how breathtaking the woman was. She was an example of divine beauty. She looked at Luke the second he decided to avert his glaze somewhere else. Luke was so caught up in the moment that he forgot that his face was in the healing phase, but Luke knew he couldn't back out now.

"That's a pretty good book." Luke didn't know what else to say. He felt so insecure about his bruised face that Luke felt like running out of the store. His clothes weren't up to par either. Luke wore his usual black, dingy hooded sweatshirt and faded blue jeans. Luke's Yankee hat covered his unkempt, misshapen mane of hair. He felt like a piece of shit.

She smiled, revealing evenly spaced teeth. "Wow, you read this? I read *The DiVinci Code* and *have* to get it."

"What can I say? Reading is my passion. What is your name by the way?"

"Zora. Zora May. And yours?"

"Luke Law. It is an outstanding pleasure to meet you Ms. May." Luke shook her hand gently.

She giggled. "Zora. I'm only twenty-eight. I'm not old yet."

A petite, caramel toned Spanish woman, her long curly hair was tied in a ponytail. Her tanned skin was creamy. Freckles covered a small portion of Zora's heart-shaped face. She wore a pair of jean shorts, and a short t-shirt that exposed her pierced naval. Zora's short t-shirt outlined her perky breasts. She spoke like a true New York Latino. English was her second language. Zora planned on improving her life through educational means. She worked as a dental receptionist, and she had been employed at the office for two months while taking two online classes in Human Services. Zora left Queens, New York abruptly due to her mother's encouragement.

"I would've never imagined you being twenty-eight. Wow," Luke said.

"Really? That's so sweet of you! Thanks. I do my best."

"Excuse my appearance. Bad things sometimes happen to good people. Unfortunately, I was one of them."

"No worries. We live in a barbaric world loaded with morally debased people."

Luke thought of the demonic look Ike wore on his face when he introduced him to three deteriorating thugs who owed, or misplaced Ike's money. Zora had inadvertently triggered Luke's flashback, but he kept a smile on his beaten face. Luke hoped Zora wasn't just being nice, and giving conversation or attention to a man that seemed like he needed it. Luke feared rejection more than he feared Ike, and being murdered. Luke didn't want her to leave. His attraction to her grew the more Zora spoke. Luke didn't cut her off one time while Zora talked; instead, he regarded every word she said like a soft melody. Zora was the sweetest human being he'd come across in years. Luke figured if he asked for Zora's number, it would be a bit premature. He decided to be patient and see where their conversation would take them. After all, Luke had a lot of time to kill, and he definitely needed a kind soul to soothe him in his time of trouble.

"So are you from up here? I never seen you around."

"Because I'm from Queens. I just moved up here a few months ago."

"What made you want to move up here to Waterbury from Queens?"

"Because a trail of money landed here for me," she chuckled and resumed. "A job. I was unemployed for a year because I got laid off from my previous employer. I posted for a job here, and I got it. What's *your* story?"

Luke could feel his heartbeat. Zora's eye contact was intense. It seemed like she stared directly into the core of Luke's soul. He was intimidated because of her beauty. Talisha was mediocre. Luke only pulled mediocre women. Dan always joked that Luke dated women who looked exactly alike. Zora was breathtaking, and she was multiple notches over every woman Luke had dated in the past. Luke did, however, mentally prepare himself for rejection or disappointment. She could be the type of woman who was naturally kind, and had a strong appreciation for humanity. Or she could be one of Ike's invisible people. When that thought crept into his head, it almost made him sick. Luke figured he would play it out with her.

"I worked at a group home that houses three patients. Last week, one of them died. Now they got us out of work pending investigation."

"Oh my gosh, that's terrible. It's probably protocol because it's an investigation. Are *you* just on leave, or are there others?"

Luke smiled.

"No, I had nothing to do with that man's death. You can be more blunt with me than that."

"Only if you can be blunt with yourself." She looked directly into Luke's war-ridden face. Luke nodded.

"So Zora, how does your day look? Busy? Kids?"

"Busy? Yes. Kids? None. Why? What about you?"

"I'll be busy later on, but right now, I'm straight. And yes, I have a nine-month-old son."

"His mother?"

"Ain't shit. You hungry?"

"I could eat. Maybe you can provide me with a baby mamma drama story," she laughed and continued. "Am I safe?"

"Yes you are; I assure you. Where would you like to go?" Luke shot himself in the foot because his car was fucked up, and there was a chance they'd get stuck. Luke rather pay a little extra to avoid *that* embarrassment.

"IHOP sound okay?"

"Sounds tasty to me," Luke said. IHOP was in the same plaza. Luke was relieved that he didn't need to transport an angel in his death trap of a vehicle.

CHAPTER 7

DEAN BONVISSUTO COULDN'T BELIEVE how lucky he was to muster the strength to ask Mary Ann out when they met at *Humphreys* last week. At the moment, however, Dean was at a loss of words. He ran his hand over his red, wild bushy hair as he gazed into Mary Ann's piercing, slanted blue eyes. Her face was round, and she had thin lips. Mary Ann's skin was tanned, and it gave off an exotic look. Her long curly brown mane touched the small of her back. Casually dressed in skinny jeans and a black, short sleeve shirt, Mary Ann was twenty-three, short, petite, and well spoken. She was eye candy and could get any male's attention, but Dean was happy Mary Ann picked him out of all the men who could only dream of going out with such a trophy. Since Dean never had any official luck with women worth sightseeing, he was surprised that he was in Mary Ann's presence. Dean believed that she was completely out of his league, but something about him attracted her. Dean figured that it had to be his size. At six foot even, Dean had the build of a light heavyweight prizefighter. Dean never thought himself to be handsome. His wild mane covered his square shaped head. His small brown eyes looked like two small dots. Dean always wore a five o'clock shadow on his face, and his skin was ruddy. He wore Old Navy jean shorts, and a tight Washington National t-shirt. Although Dean viewed his physical appearance as a personal shortcoming, he was well compensated in another area...money. Dean's parents were wealthy anthropologists, and they were currently in South Africa digging in the dirt for million dollar fossils and artifacts. Dean's parents were scheduled to remain overseas for the next three months. Dean's parents wired him money once a week, about five hundred dollars since he didn't work. The money was supposed to cover the basics, and a little fuck around money. Dean took the money and used it to start his ecstasy pill business, which was lucrative. When he wasn't in summer classes at Southern Connecticut State University or studying, Dean oversaw the growth of his business. Dean flipped that money tenfold by selling ecstasy tablets that looked like bronze and gold-colored Athenian tetradrachms that had Mark Antony and Cleopatra imprinted on them. Dean made a ton of money. His area of study was mathematics with a minor in politics. He applied his specialty and his calling to a dirty business that increased his bank.

Dean's parent's well-landscaped waterfront house was situated on the shoreline in Branford, Connecticut. It had six bedrooms, four bathrooms, an exercise room, a movie theater, and a tennis court. A rear and upper deck overlooked an in-ground swimming pool. Dean's parents were loaded. He only went to school in Connecticut, but Dean and his parents' main residence was in Helene, Montana. They owned a few homes on the east coast.

Dean and Mary Ann sat with their legs folded together in the middle of the expensively furnished and decorated living room. They asked each other questions. They had good conversation about history, but politics prevailed over the two-way interrogation.

Mary Ann smiled, moved her hair to the side, and clapped her hands excitedly. "Okay, ask me another one. This is fun."

"I think we shouldn't talk anymore about politics. It's a dirty, scandalous topic that I happen to enjoy. I don't want to leave a disgusting impression on our first night together," Dean said.

"No, I doubt that. My skin may be soft, but it's thick. Try me. Don't be such a wuss. I love a gentleman that owns his own opinion."

Dean melted as he gazed at Mary Ann's smile and her dimples.

"Ok, you asked for it." Dean readjusted his posture, picked up his pipe, lit the weed, and inhaled deeply.

"What do you think of the state's budget?"

"I think it sucks," Mary Ann said. She accepted the lighter and the pipe from Dean. "I think its sucks that the middle class are always taking the biggest sacrifice, but politicians call it *shared* sacrifice." Mary

Ann placed her hands in the air and waved two fingers from both hands, and indicated that the term *share sacrifice* was bullshit.

Dean felt more comfortable with each passing minute. He never expressed his opinionated output on *any* subject because Dean hated the idea of not being liked because of the view he had on life.

"With all due respect, and I really mean no pun intended, when was the last time a poor or middle class person gave you a job? Never," Dean said, answering his own question with a glimpse of haughty arrogance. "You have all these...state workers with no education making wages where they'll be able to share the same golf course as my dad. Meanwhile, I'm busting my ass in school trying to make a little higher salary than someone who never had to use their brain?"

The expression on Mary Ann's face didn't change. "My friend Jennifer is a clinical social worker. A degree is required for that position. I believe she has a master's degree."

Dean shook his head. "No Mary Ann, I'm talking about the frontline jobs; the jobs that only require a high school diploma. *Come on* Mary Ann. Those jobs are not *that* dangerous for them to be bringing home that much bacon, and to receive the best benefit package known to mankind. I say they should lay them all off, and hire some immigrants who would work for twelve to fifteen bucks an hour."

"Dean, I know nothing of those jobs, but I know one thing; children shouldn't have to suffer because of a state's need to save a few million bucks. The tech schools are going to suffer behind all of this."

"Believe me, I went to a tech school, and the only thing teachers teach is the basic foundation of electrical, plumbing, auto, and carpentry. Technology changes every day, making these crafts more advanced. A student in the school of carpentry would be lucky to half-way know how to use a saw."

Mary Ann shrugged her shoulders. "Point well taken Dean, but with a collapsed economy, who is going to buy your stupid pills?"

"Then I'll turn them all to pill heads, make them fiends," Dean said, mocking a black man he saw recently on a low budget gangster film. "No, I'm just kidding. And speaking of addiction, my craving for pizza exceeded far beyond a half hour. I'm not giving them a tip."

"Cheapskate," Mary Ann said good-naturedly. "Your parents shit money Dean. Why do you have to risk everything you have, including your future?"

"My parents are rich, not this asshole," Dean said humorously, pointing at himself. "I'm setting up my early retirement." Dean got up, walked to the first closet in the hallway, and opened the door. He pulled out a large box, and he brought it to where Mary Ann sat. Dean sat down and opened it. There were over five thousand ecstasy pills in the box. They went for thirty a pop.

Dean put his nose up in the air, looking like a pious prick. "Once I flip these babies ten, fifteen times, I'll be on my way to living the way a king is supposed to live. I only have to put 20, 25 bucks a week in my 401k...if that."

After a few more bowl hits, someone rang the doorbell. Dean smiled, and he looked at the beautiful specimen once more before he got up from his leg-crossed position on the floor. When Dean opened the door, a short Hispanic man stood before him with a peculiar look on his face.

"You're late. How much do I owe ya?" Dean asked with an attitude. The deliveryman was late, but Dean's attitude wasn't necessary. Dean became more irate when the guy didn't answer him.

Dean looked to see what Mary Ann was doing. He didn't want her to see his racist side. "Hey Santos, what's the damage?"

"Hey Scotty, the damage are those *E* pills I know you got stashed up in there," a gruff male's voice said. The voice was coming from the side of the summer home.

Dean laughed.

"Okay Shane, cut the shit. Dude, did Alex put you up to this?"

Dean never saw the stress on the Hispanic man's oval face. The man knew little English, but the man knew Shane was a name, but didn't know anyone by it.

"What are you doing out there? Negotiating? Mr. Mathematical Genius, I'm starving."

Dean turned around.

"I'm coming," Dean chuckled, looking stupid. "I'm just dealing with some uninvited guests."

NEXT OF KIN

By the time Dean turned around, a medium sized man who wore a black ski mask stood before Dean. He pointed a Smith and Wesson Night Guard .44 directly at his face. Another man who wore a red ski mask held the deliveryman hostage. In spite of evidence to the contrary, Dean still didn't take the situation seriously. Mary Ann, on the other hand, did; her face was fixed in a mask of horror as she viewed the scene before her. Dean looked inside the barrel of the gun to see if it was a prop. When Dean lifted his hand to snatch the tool, the man in the black mask countered him with the weapon, knocking Dean to the floor, the mass of his body producing a loud thud on the kitchen tile. Dean remained conscious, and the blow changed his theory about the situation being a joke.

"Still think this is a game? Where them pills?" Black masked asked thickly.

Dean pointed to the box that sat right next to Mary Ann's leg. The box was wide opened, and filled to the brim. Dean's face spelled horror. A tear traveled down his rosy cheek. Dean's bowels moved, and liquid stool seeped from the inside of his boxers. Dean trembled, and his jaw vibrated with the rhythm of his own fear. Dean stared blankly at Mary Ann who whimpered and flinched when black mask instructed red mask to pack up the goods. Black mask went inside his extra large duffel bag, and he pulled out two rolls of rope made with synthetic fiber. Black mask expertly hogtied the man. He ignored the sight and smell of waste.

"Dude, there are over five thousand pi..."

Black mask shut him up by kicking him in the stomach.

Mary Ann looked at Dean, and she became disgusted. Dean looked pathetic as red mask tied her wrists and legs. Dean finally looked into the two holes used for eyes on the black mask, and saw the real ones. Dean couldn't see black mask's twisted smile, but Dean felt it.

"Now that we got what we came for, no one gets hurt. You can keep the shit in your pants man. But there is one more thing I want from y'all," Black Mask said.

"Haven't you guys taken enough and caused enough damage? Why don't you two leave, and go do what you guys do best like be a nuisance to someone else. You two must feel real tough with those guns and masks..."

"Please," Dean interrupted. Mary Ann's rant. He didn't want her to fuck around and get them both killed. "Let these men take whatever they want! Dude, my parents have priceless artifacts, jewelry, whatever. Just don't kill us...please!"

"Ain't that some shit? Your bitch got more heart than you do." Black Mask kicked Dean viciously in the pit of his stomach. Dean vomited.

"Kill the phones," Black Mask instructed. Red Mask took their cell phones, the deliveryman's phone included, and watered them before he stashed them in the large duffle bag.

Mary Ann looked up from her hogtied position on the floor. "I got more balls than you too. I didn't come over here with a gun."

Black Mask smiled notoriously underneath it before he proceeded in her direction. Black Mask stopped directly in front of her. She stared blankly into Black Mask's beady eyes as he began to grope her. Mary Ann's eyes followed Dean's hogtied form. Dean shivered with fear. He turned away from Mary Ann's gaze, and Dean closed his eyes, and hoped the men would do what they wanted and had to do so they could leave. If that meant raping Mary Ann, fuck it, he figured. Dean wanted to see another day.

"Time is expiring. Let's sweep and leave," the man wearing the red mask said, finally shattering the silence. Luke felt Dan went a little overboard, but the mansion was swank, and the men knew it possessed more treasure beyond those ecstasy pills.

Dan readjusted his black mask, lifted the deliveryman to his feet, and pistol-whipped him. The blow knocked him out. Dan reasoned that it was better than killing him. The crime partners left Mary Ann in the living room tied and gagged. The henchmen walked the fear stricken young drug dealer over the entire perimeter of the high-class residence. The masked men remained silent as Dean gave them access to everything valuable in the house, which included new jewelry, jewelry that had been in the family for generations, pricey artifacts, and one hundred fifty thousand dollars, the money Dean had from a previous re-up.

NEXT OF KIN

When the men left, the deliveryman displayed small signs of life as he began to regain his consciousness. Since Pedro was from the street, and had been incarcerated a few times, he knew better than to talk to the police. Pedro made it to his feet, picked up the pizza leather cover, and left the premises. As Mary Ann struggled against her bonds, she miraculously found that red mask hadn't secured her restraints properly. Dean lie in a pile of his fear-induced shit and sulked. Instead of engineering a blueprint for revenge, Dean decided to leave the game alone because he knew he wasn't built for it. Dean was an Atheist, but he thanked God that he was still alive.

CHAPTER 8

I **KE SAT ON A** plush lounge chair at the Borgata in the Piatto suite being flanked by two women. One of the women, tall and voluptuous, was dark skinned, and she wore a weave that extended down to her shoulders. The woman was crouched between Ike's knees. She sucked on the shaft of Ike's penis. There wasn't a single dent or dimple on her toned body. Her *D* sized breasts were firm and her dark areolas were pointed to the floor as she gagged on his girth.

The tall dark skinned woman's friend, a light skin Cape Verdean with fake, thick eyelashes, sat behind Ike, and she rubbed Ike's sculpted body while he enjoyed his blowjob. The Cape Verdean woman was short and petite with fake, *C* sized breasts that accentuated her thin waist. Ike was suddenly jarred from the haze of his pleasure by a sharp knock on the door of the suite. Annoyed, Ike beckoned the women to get off of him.

"For heaven's sake, who is it?"

"It's me Boss."

"Who's me? I lead plenty of you," Ike said arrogantly. He knew exactly who it was.

"Toby."

Ike rose from his seat with his dick fully erect, and he walked across the plush carpet. Ike peered out of the peephole for safe measure before he opened the door. Toby stood at the door like an obedient dog. Toby held a duffle bag full of greenbacks collected from thugs who knew better than to hold out. Toby was prepared to take whatever order Ike demanded. When Ike walked away from the door after he opened it, with the duffle bag in hand, Toby waited for Ike to invite him in. While Toby waited, he took in the entire suite, and Toby knew that his feet would never had touched the carpet he was standing on if it wasn't for Ike. Stone vases held exotic plants, and they were spread strategically throughout the suite. Imported marble vanities and floor to ceiling windows overlooked the entire city, which included a breath-taking view of the Atlantic Ocean and its beach. Half-empty wine glasses stood on top of the circular glass table. Two of the glasses were decorated with lipstick. The small vase on the table was loaded with pink, red, and white mums. A flat screen television was bolted to one of the walls.

Ike looked at Toby, and signaled him inside. The two women were naked, and they didn't bother to cover themselves. Toby had seen countless thirsty, money hungry naked women in Ike's presence, but the women didn't look familiar.

Toby was behind Ike's naked rear end while Ike's dick grazed the dresser the drinks were on. Ike combined coconut Ciroc and Sprite. Toby stood stone-faced behind him, not moving a single facial muscle as he waited for Ike to speak. Ike gave Toby and the women a drink without saying a word and stood, naked as the day he was born, smiled, and held up his glass towards the brute of a man. The women followed his lead.

"Cheers to Toby, a good gentlemen who can abruptly ruin a climax.".

"Cheers," the women said in unison.

Toby smirked and threw back his full drink as if it was a shot. The women laughed at Toby as they whispered insults amongst each other. Toby gave them a cold look, and the women stopped. Toby was docile around Ike, but everyone else was fair game. Toby killed many men and women and wouldn't mind if Ike gave him permission to choke out the bitches. Toby may be inferior in life and pose no significance in society, but he could make the best of them disappear. Toby was a certified coldhearted killer.

Ike sat between the two nude women, and played with them as if Toby wasn't in the room. Sex noises and moans escaped the trio's mouths as they fell deeper into their lust. Toby grew a little irate about Ike's cocky demeanor, but Toby would never express it. Ike was the only man alive who had ever taken care of him. Toby felt rejected by the rest of the world since the day he slipped out of the womb.

"Toby, are you going to watch, or are you going to stand there and provide no utterance of the status at hand. You're being tedious," Ike said as he circled his tongue around the Cape Verdean woman's dark nipple.

"With these bitches in here?" Toby asked as if the women were domesticated animals. They ignored Toby, and they pleasured each other and Ike.

Ike ignored Toby as well. Ike inserted two fingers into the dark skinned chick's pussy. She moaned and gyrated her hips against Ike's fingers while he kissed her softly from her cheek to her areolas.

"Toby," Ike said while he indulged in his own lust. "Add another tool in the garage. A general deterrence doesn't seem to work anymore." Ike started to run his tongue over the dark skinned woman's naval. She bit her bottom lip. "No more warnings. It's *actus reus* all the way. Our adversaries in debt don't quite seem to understand memos."

"Done Ike. Consider it the past," Toby said while he shot a glance at the women, and still couldn't figure out why Ike talked around the strangers. Toby started to go with his gut, but he figured the broads were dumb hood chicks that couldn't understand what Ike said anyway. Toby wasn't going to question him about it.

"Teddy's right hand man been stealing from you Ike."

Ike's head was tilted back on the couch with his mouth wide opened, moaning, and steeped in ecstasy when he released his semen in the mouth of the Cape Verdean. She sucked him off until Ike's dick lost its erection. Toby wasn't sure if Ike processed what he said, but Toby knew Ike had heard him loud and clear.

After the women separated themselves from Ike, and got into the bed, Ike got up from the couch, semen all over the shaft of his penis, and walked to the dresser and poured himself and Toby another drink.

"How much?" Ike finally asked.

"Five thousand so far."

Ike paraded a sinister grin. "Pennies.Let him take a little more before we crack down on him. He's a kid, but he's old enough to get a tour of the dungeon, the last tour he'll ever proceed on. Any who, what about Mr. Law?"

NEXT OF KIN

"Not much as of yet boss, but he is moving along. He got his thugged out homie ridin' wit' em. I kept a small tail on him. He's a drug dealer. He hangs out at this local bar in some hood they call *the bowl*. He ain't hard to find."

Ike pulled out a pair of black silk boxers, gray jeans, and a black Polo sweater and carefully laid them across the couch. Ike left Toby standing there in the presence of the women while he showered and shaved. Under Ike, one was always on the clock. Ike had thousands of dollars worth of jewelry, and he left Toby there to watch it. After Ike emerged from the shower and got dressed, Ike resumed his thoughts about Luke.

"I don't give a rat's rear about the kind of action Mr. Law is taking to obtain my physical equivalent. Is he persistent? Studies have shown that people under duress, people who have their backs against the wall, infested with fear, tend to work above and beyond their regular brain capacity. If that theory holds true, then he's on his way to repaying me his brother's debt, but if he needs his aggressive drug dealing counterpart to aid him on his do or die journey, so be it."

Toby watched his superior through cold, slanted eyes as Ike proceeded as if all the hard work and long hours he put in on Luke meant nothing. Toby tracked, enforced, and killed for Ike, and got a pretty penny for it, but Toby felt he needed a pat on the back every now then.

"He puttin' in work...he and his boy robbed..."

Ike rummaged meticulously through his bag. "Means nothing to me. It doesn't matter how or what Mr. Law is doing just as long as he is doing it." With that said, Toby turned to walk away.

"And Toby, good job for your performance," Ike said. He knew his inferior well. Toby wanted a compliment. Compliments were huge for Toby because he didn't receive them often in his life. "Before you go back to Connecticut," Ike leaned and got close to Toby's ear, "take out the trash." Ike shot a glance at the smug women engaged in a sixty nine.

Toby looked confused.

"The dark skinned one. Her husband, Javon Wadsworth, my favorite NBA superstar, dropped my name in the court of law during his heyday as a flunky. I believe you know this already, and him running from the safe house after it was robbed. You know the rest of that situation. He avoided my calls, and as you see, I love being the center of attention." Ike glanced at the women again. "Her friend is just at the wrong place at the wrong time. Kill them."

Toby nodded his head, still energized by Ike's comment about his job performance. Toby's gut feeling earlier about the women's potential deaths was confirmed. He remembered when the women laughed and talked shit. Toby was delighted.

With the simple wave of Ike's hand, Toby was dismissed, commissioned to inflict death, and ordered back to Connecticut.

CHAPTER 9

LUKE LAY ON HIS bed and contemplated his next move two weeks after he lost his virginity to robbery. There was an absence of sound in the apartment, but the cars, trucks, pedestrians, and motorcycles added a little life to it. As usual, just like any other Friday night, Talisha was in a night club. That was the *least* of Luke's worries. He had Baron, his mother, and his own life to be worried about. Ever since he found the semen stains on Talisha's leg, Luke found it hard to warn her that her life, too, was in danger. Luke didn't wish death on anyone, but he would have sacrificed Talisha to wipe out Steve's debt. A jolt of guilt crashed into his mind, but he couldn't stand her.

Finally, Luke got out of the bed. He retrieved the loaded Ruger he kept stashed underneath his pillow, and he walked to the kitchen with it in hand in case of a surprise. After he poured himself a beverage, Luke stood at his kitchen counter, a grim look ingrained on his face while he suffered a bout of uncertainty. Luke knew he needed a bag of strength for the sake of his family. Dan was the key to Luke's capers; however, Luke knew he needed to be creative. After all, Dan had his own share of problems, but Luke needed a lic. He needed one fast. Luke began to pace the kitchen. He felt mixed emotions about his life-altering ordeal. Luke's days had been murky since his brutal ultimatum; moreover, his paranoia had skyrocketed to the maximum. The distance between him and Talisha had climaxed, but with each day that passed, Luke became less frightened of his situation, and he quietly grew more hardened. While Luke paced, he couldn't help but smile at the look the white dude had on his face when he and Dan robbed him. When the man shitted on himself, Luke felt a sense of power, a power he'd never experienced. Despite the changes in his personality, Ike's threat on his family, and the memories of the bodies woke him up abruptly every day.

Luke stepped out onto the third floor porch to smoke a blunt. With the gun tucked into his waistband, Luke inhaled deeply, and wondered who was at work at the group home, and then it finally hit him. The lic Luke sought was underneath his nose all along. Luke decided to go back to his roots. After he smoked the blunt, Luke walked back inside the apartment, and looked at his set of keys. Bingo. Luke still had the key to his place of employment. Luke made the biggest stack of his life when he and Dan flipped the ecstasy pills. He thought about all the controlled meds double locked in the medication closet. Luke's job disrespected him when they removed him from his post, and declared him guilty until proven innocent. Luke's employer had some revenge coming their way.

Luke hoped it was Murphy that worked the night shift instead of Jackson. The reason being had nothing to do with friendship. Murphy had no children, wife, or life. Jackson was a father of four, and his wife had been laid off from her employer. Luke personally liked Jackson, but whoever was at work tonight would be in an investigation tomorrow. Regardless, Luke was coming after those pills.

Luke coasted down the Southington Mountain on his moped through heavy wind, gust, drizzle, and fog. The weather was warm, but Mother Nature's attitude was nasty on that June night. Luke coasted slowly. Going faster on the slippery terrain on a moped could prove fatal. He slowed the moped to a crawl, veered left, and jetted down a side street loaded with trees that swayed in the turbulent wind. Once Luke was off the side street, he rode his moped quietly through streets occupied by mansions, Georgia, German, New England colonials, ranches, split-level, and Victorian "Gingerbread" houses.

Only a few houses away from the group home, Luke's heartbeat skyrocketed. He got off the moped, walked it through a small patch of woods, hid it out of sight, and stealthily made moves up the neighbor's driveway. Luke knew the neighbors had motion lights so he carried extra caution, moving to the center of the driveway. Luke took a right into the wild weeds and shrubbery. He sighed a breath of relief when he saw Murphy's car instead of Jackson's vehicle. Murphy falls asleep one hour into third shift, which was a plus. Motion lights surrounded the home, but to Luke's surprise, they were off. Luke walked around the perimeter to the backyard, and then onto the deck. Darkness flooded the kitchen and living room. Luke didn't expect staff to be upstairs. The noise from the television would wake up the patients. Luke put on a pair of rubber gloves, and he tried the sliding door. It was locked. He tried other methods of entry into the home without the use of keys. Luke cursed because the sliding door was less risky. He walked around to the front of the house. Luke peeped through the basement window. Murphy was asleep with his mouth opened in front of the television. Luke headed toward the garage door, and to his delight, he found it ajar. He lifted it slowly, and he wormed himself in. Luke left it cracked for an easy escape.

Murphy's snoring filled the small hallway with noise. Careful not to make the steps squeak, Luke moved hurriedly, took two lefts, and went into the office. The keys to the medication closet were on the desk in plain view. When Luke stuck the key into the doorknob, the new client that replaced the deceased one darted past the office, and down the stairs. Luke curse, put the key back on the desk, ran across the hall, and hid himself underneath the new client's bed where his nose met and were greeted by soiled adult diapers. Luke covered his nose with his sweatshirt. He tried to block the putrid smell. He heard Murphy move up the stairs, probably to get the new client a PRN for some type of disturbed behavior. Luke heard Murphy opening the medication boxes, and popping pills out of their bubble packs. Five minutes came and went and Murphy was still reading instructions on a pack. Luke began to sweat. He heard Murphy leave a message for the on-call nurse to call back. Luke knew the on-call nurse was Gloria, and that she took her time calling back whenever her expertise was needed.

Twenty-five minutes later, the bitch finally called back. Murphy told her instructions were not provided for the administration of the patient's Ativan that was to be given as a PRN (as needed). After a few more minutes of small talk, Murphy and Gloria parted ways. Murphy gave the client the Ativan and went back downstairs. The client went back to bed.

Luke waited a few more minutes before taking action. Just when he prepared to make a move from underneath the bed, the client shuffled and groaned before he screamed loudly. Murphy walked up the stairs, opened the door, and told the client to shut the fuck up and go back to bed before he slammed the door.

Luke was beyond sweating, and he wanted to rip and run quickly. The client was on his bullshit again. The patient grunted and made noises with his mouth. Luke came from underneath the bed, stood up, and pistol-whipped him into unconsciousness. Luke stepped out of the room hastily, heard Murphy's movement, and went back underneath the bed. Murphy opened the door, flashed the LED light on the client, and walked back down the stairs. Luke endured more of the stench under the bed to be safe.

Luke came from underneath the bed, went into the medication closet, and swiped it clean. He was drenched with sweat when he carefully made his way back downstairs. Murphy was on the couch asleep. On ground level, Luke was in the clear, but Murphy's wallet caught his attention because it bulged with hundreds and fifties. Under any circumstances, Luke would never steal another man's money, but tonight wasn't no ordinary circumstance. Luke snatched the cash, and darted out of the group home without incident.

CHAPTER 10

AT 7:30 IN THE MORNING, the sunshine and the torrid heat was a far cry from the intense downpour last night. Luke and Dan waited for their breakfast at *Brass City Diner*. Luke gave Dan the details of last night's lift. The unimpressed, withered, old Caucasian blond waitress approached their table with beverages. The men resumed the conversation when the waitress walked away.

"That's what it be fam. You did what you had to do. You hear anything about it since you pulled it off?" Dan asked.

"Yeah, the dude that was working last night can't come back to work until the situation is settled, but fuck it. I'd rather him lose his job than me losing my life, you feel me?"

Dan nodded after he set his orange juice down.

"I would say lets go after the other group homes, but right now, we got to fall back on that shit. Your agency might fuck around and invest in around the clock surveillance. And just so you'll know, you and the other motherfuckers that's out pending investigation are going to be the prime suspects. Did you glove up?"

Luke looked at Dan incredulously.

"Just askin' fam. You could never be too safe. Since those other group homes is out the picture for right now, I got a new lick, but it's risky as fuck."

"Lay it on me," Luke said.

"Chill fam. Lets grub first. I told her we would meet at her crib for further discussion."

Luke contorted his face in a mask of confusion.

"Her? Did I meet this chick?"

Dan chuckled. "You never met her personally, but you seen her. She the reason why we took that ride to Southbury that night after we hit your mom's crib."

"How risky is this lick bro? Lives? Prison?" Luke's face soured.

"Nigga, anything illegal we do is risky, but if this shit is done incorrectly, all of the above. This particular lick is like a nigga standing six inches away from the prison holding a boulder."

A stream of worry went straight to Luke's stomach, but he'd managed not to let Dan in on his fear. Dan was going to say something, but the unenthused waitress arrived at the table with their breakfast. The men devoured their breakfast with little conversation, paid the bill, and left the diner to link up with Dan's third-party member.

Dan drove around the corner, and up Mark Lane through the condominiums that were once occupied by the upper class, but within the last few decades or so, the complex had slowly deteriorated. The men waited patiently outside of one of the units. They heard footsteps. She opened the door, and left it opened. It was the white girl from the ecstasy robbery. Dan set the shit up. Luke looked at Dan in bewilderment; Dan replied with a smirk.

Open space filled the living room. Only an office chair, two folding chairs, notebook, and a nineteen-inch Panasonic flat screen decorated the living room. Luke only knew the woman as a victim, and as Mary Ann, but Luke recognized her by her eyes.

"It took you long enough. I have shit to do just like you," she said with an attitude. She walked in the kitchen, and reappeared with an astray and a blunt inside of it. Her sour attitude was directed at Dan.

"Luke, Rosa, Rosa, Luke. Now lets get to business." Dan ignored Rosa's attitude.

"Daniel, please don't do that. I'm already irritated with you. Stop disrespecting my time. You're carrying on as if what I have to say is worthless."

"You're absolutely right Rosa, really, but right now, you don't know or understand the magnitude of anything, so just chill so we can discuss, plan, and get paid."

"Whatever." She took the blunt out of the ashtray and sparked it. Luke invited himself to a folding chair. Dan and Rosa had something going on, but the two spoke business without any emotional outbursts. Rosa didn't conduct herself like the tough white chick that grew some heart during a hold-up. She spoke like a seasoned career criminal. Larceny was embedded in Rosa's heart. Talks about the reality of their pockets, taking action, and getting paid was all good, but when Dan mentioned sticking up an armory truck, Luke's hopes and dreams went out the window. Luke was shook, and Rosa took note of it.

"This has to be fast and fluid, and with all due respect, your boy needs to take that hesitant shit out of his step."

That grabbed Luke's attention.

"What?"

"You heard me. The whole ecstasy drop...you were stiff. This is way more riskier than that elementary shit we pulled off."

"Watch how you come out of your face; you don't know me like that." Luke was getting pissed.

"I know a rookie when I see one. I normally call a spade a spade."

"Rosa, chill," Dan interjected.

"Chill nothing. I'm not going back to jail, and not over his scary ass."

"Dan, tell this bitch something. I don't know who the fuck you think you are!"

Rosa shot Luke a furious glance. "Who are you calling a bitch?"

"Rosa, shut that shit up! Stop trying to cause a problem. If you have an issue, take it up like a professional and address it later, but don't be comin' at my nigga like that, and you don't know him from a fuckin' hole in the wall."

"Fine Dan, whatever you say, but you and I know the deal. He needs to loosen up."

"Are you done?" Dan was getting impatient with her.

"I said what I had to say. And i..."

"Ok." Dan cut her off. "Luke, real talk, timing is everything, so we all need to be on point. And speaking of which, handle your business Rosa. I'll see you tonight." Dan kissed her softly, but she shot daggers at Luke before she went into the kitchen. The men left without saying another word.

In the car, Dan apologized for Rosa's actions, but also acknowledged that Rosa hustled, boosted, and set people up for years. She treated her craft as a true profession, and that she had a right to be paranoid.

"And by the way, she's pregnant. Just found out yesterday."

"Damn Dan, Rhonda know?"

"Nope," Dan said. "And that's the way it will stay."

Luke had his own problems. "It's none of my business, bro, and you know me better than that."

"That's why I told you," Dan said. Luke was the only one he trusted.

CHAPTER 11

CHEERFUL AND TALKATIVE, Zora enjoyed herself and Luke's company at Red Lobster on the Silas Dean Highway. Luke remained silent, and his smile was forced. Luke's bland demeanor had nothing to do with Zora, and she never picked up on it. Luke perfected a massive front to conceal his darkly, fearful mood. He was grateful that Zora couldn't see the pain he masked.

Luke learned a lot about Zora. She shared a lot about herself despite it being their first date. Listening attentively, Luke learned she was lonely, and in need of attention. Zora did, however, confess that while Luke's bruises were a red flag, his personality, handsome features, and innocent, tranquil demeanor piqued her interest.

Luke enjoyed her. If he wasn't so hyper vigilant, Luke be head over heels, and more engaged. His attention was focused on the threat of harm that Ike and Toby presented, while Zora chatted away, oblivious to the danger that Luke was vulnerable to. Zora was a beautiful woman with creamy flesh, and her manner of speech was soft spoken. Luke could hardly tolerate the thought that someone he was so attracted to, and could possibly grow to love could be harmed because of his associations.

"Hello, Earth to Luke. Hello." Luke snapped himself out of his fog, and shifted his attention back to her.

"I heard you," he said easily, brushing his morbid, dark thoughts aside to regain a little of his focus. "I'm a Taurus, but personally, I don't believe in signs. My horoscope may be horrible in the Waterbury Republican, but it may say I'm going to be rich in the horoscopes in the New York Times."

Zora giggled.

"Yes Luke, I agree, but I'm talking about personality traits. Since I'm a Cancer, I connect emotionally to people. Every Cancer I know can reciprocate emotions on any level. I knew you were a Taurus when we first met."

Luke smiled and took a swig of his Heineken.

"And how did you know that?" Luke set his gaze on her. Zora's curly hair was draped over her shoulders, her eyes dreamy and mysterious, and her leg crossed over the other one. She looked like a painter's masterpiece.

All of a sudden, Luke was caught off guard. Luke spotted one of the very men who haunted his thoughts. There, in a Dodge Avenger, was Toby. If Luke hadn't sat near the window, he wouldn't had noticed the murderous thug. Luke panicked; his gun was in the car, but he carried his knife. Bold, bearded, and huge, Toby met Luke's gaze. Fear dripped through Luke's body. Toby sensed it from the parking lot, and he enjoyed every minute of it. Zora continued to chatter away, oblivious to Luke's discovery. Luke forced himself to shift his attention back to Zora. She never stopped the conversation.

"I hope I'm not being a chatter box. I'm always up front and expressive."

Luke forced a smile, and placed his hands over hers.

"There is nothing wrong with being up front Zora. I expect nothing short of it." Luke peered out the window again, but there was no trace of the burly son of a bitch. The timing was perfect. They completed their meals. Toby made his arrival at the conclusion of it. It was time to make moves.

"I have one question for you," Zora said.

Luke's mind raced. Zora seemed comfortable, and in a zone. He didn't want to rush the night, but the last time he saw Toby, Luke saw several fully street clothed cadavers in an abandoned factory. He couldn't put an innocent woman in potential danger. Luke didn't want her caught in the crosshair of any type of destruction.

"Shoot."

"Your girlfriend."

"My who?"

"The mother of your child. How do you think she would feel if she found out that you were in the company of another woman?"

"Considering I saw dried semen on her thigh after sneaking in the bed one morning, I don't care how she feels. Don't worry Zora; I would never put you in harm's way."

"That's too bad," she said while she effortlessly tied her hair up with an elastic band.

Luke and Zora had another round of drinks. Toby continued to roam around in the parking lot while Luke tried to watch him, and give Zora attention at the same time.

"I don't mean to end our night prematurely, but I think its time we head out. I have to work in the morning," Zora said.

Relieved that he didn't have to come up with a lie, Luke nodded his head before he flagged the waitress down for the check. After the transaction and tip, the pair walked out of the restaurant locked in each other's arm. Luke had his free hand on the shell of the blade he carried. They walked to the car and separated when they reached it.

Luke coasted on I-91 south. Traffic flowed smoothly; the light Jazz seeped softly through the speakers. Zora closed her eyes, and she enjoyed the music. Luke was paranoid, and he checked his rearview mirror repeatedly. Zora began to speak of signs, mood, and emotions. When she dug a little into her background, Toby appeared in the rearview mirror when he got off the Scott Road exit. Luke remained calm. The fuzz pulled over every other vehicle so they can do checks. Zora started to ramble, but he kept his focus on the Lincoln MKX. Luke blew a sigh of relief when Toby proceeded dangerously off the exit. He drove over a rough patch of terrain, and back unto the highway. Luke was so engaged in his relief that he didn't know Zora tried to get his attention.

"Luke, are you listening to me?"

He turned to face her.

"I hope your situation at home is what you say it is. If I could take a guess, I would say that you think she is following us."

She didn't notice Luke's odd behavior until now. Luke brainstormed.

"Ha, ha, no Zora, I told you the truth from the jump," he said. "Talisha is the last one you need to worry about. I'm not perfect, but

I'm not a liar. If my son weren't in the picture, she would have *been* out. A child complicates the hell out of things."

Zora allowed her hair to drape over her shoulders before she pulled it back up into a ponytail. "What about other situations?"

Gassed and flattered, Luke couldn't believe a woman of Zora's caliber paid him time and day. Luke wondered more about her, and wished he paid her more attention at the restaurant, but Luke's life was more important.

"There are absolutely no other situations Zora. You could be one if you'd like."

She smiled. Luke wished he were able to take back what he said. He wanted her, but he didn't need her to indirectly step into a crosshair.

They missed the road check by a car. The ride to Zora's home was quiet. Luke didn't want to write Toby off because he could be anywhere. As expected, Zora sat and spoke about the bullshit and gossip about her job like he worked there. The sound of Zora's voice was heaven, but since he was packed with fear, Luke wanted her out the car. Even though he was fear-stricken, Luke still wanted her. Her personality was bright, but Zora's light could be permanently darkened if she hung around.

"I know I'm talking your ear off, but I don't know anyone from here. I only been here a few months, and have not befriended a soul, but thank you for this evening. I really enjoyed myself." She gathered her belongings. After they hugged tightly, they positioned their faces in front of one another, their lips a half-inch apart, and they kissed. Zora wrapped her arms around Luke, and she stroked the back of his head while engaged in a blissful kiss. They separated slowly. Zora smiled radiantly before she left the car. She blew a kiss, and disappeared behind her apartment door. Luke pulled off, hung a right, and escaped to the main road.

Toby wasn't going to hurt Luke tonight, but Toby wanted his presence felt. He wanted Luke to know that he would die if he couldn't come up with his brother's debt. Toby rode down Zora's street, unaware that his prey had slipped away from him, and that Luke's new interest lived on the second floor of the three-family home he drove by.

CHAPTER 12

THE EARLY MORNING AIR was warm and provided no hint of rain, but promised a day of heat. Luke sat in the passenger seat of the Range Rover and provided Dan with the cliff note's version of last night's date with Zora, and Toby's guest appearance. Dan bashed Luke for not having his gun on him in the restaurant, and theorized that Toby's appearance was a "don't catch amnesia" scenario. If Toby wanted to snatch and kill Luke, he would be dead by now. The men continued to small talk, and they killed more time before they handled their business.

"Quincy sent me a letter addressed to you at my crib," Dan said.

"He don't know my current address, but he know my mom's joint. That dude been down too long."

"Or maybe your mother sends the letters back to where they came from," Dan said.

"Nah. She would just give me the correspondence."

"True. I'll give you that later, but for now, we need to handle this business."

The digital clock on the deck read 3am. The men were parked two streets away from the target. They waited for the right time to strike. Luke worked in the group home sparingly. He knew the group home contained seven types of controlled medication. Luke and Dan drove to Meriden to burglarize, but if the occupants were not cooperative, it could turn into a robbery. They masked themselves, grabbed the tools for bondage, closed the trunk, and started the mission. Dan began to question the escape route, but Luke told him they were not going to walk the next street; they were going to cut through someone's yard to decrease the length of the escape route.

Luke and Dan stealthily crept alongside a one level home. When they arrived in the backyard, a Rottweiler growled at them. The dog could sense that his owners were in danger. The men stood frozen, but Dan planned ahead. The chained dog charged at them at full speed, the dog's mouth dripping saliva and malicious intent, anxious to get at the intruders. The dog shortened the gap and his leash was long. There was enough slack in the chain for the dog to travel to the front yard, but the men were in the backyard, in the core of hostile territory. The canine barked, lunged, and landed on the masked duo, but the dog yelped after Dan drove the blade through the dog's skull. The dog squealed and shook ferociously before he drew his last breath. Luke vomited and Dan stood over the dog with his mouth open, relieved he and Luke weren't the victims.

"Lets get this motherfucker out of view. I hope nobody didn't hear that shit," Luke whispered.

The men dragged the dead dog out of view, and waited a few minutes. Luke flinched when Dan pulled the knife out of the deceased dog's head. Dan wiped the dog's coat with its own blood. He felt bad for the dog that only protected its territory, but it was necessary.

Crouched against the company vehicle, Luke equipped his right hand with a jawbreaker. If the weapon was used to it's full potential, it could kill. That was not the intent; however, Luke simply meant to knock his potential victim out from third shift until the start of first.

"If one of those patients wake up, knock 'em out. Sometimes we can't avoid collateral damage Luke. It's part of the game. If motherfuckers stay in they place, they won't..."

Adam, a lard white dude who snitched constantly, stepped onto the porch, dug into his pockets, fetched a light, and lit his Camel cigarette. The men watched Adam, and they waited for the perfect opportunity to temporarily put him out of commission. When Adam was almost finished with his cancer stick, Luke started to move slowly in his direction. Adam took another drag of his cigarette, and he smashed it in the standing ashtray. When Adam's hand touched the doorknob to resume his work duties, his sight turned to black. Luke caught him square on the jaw.

NEXT OF KIN

Samantha, an Italian brunette who wore skinny jeans and a "Life Sucks" t-shirt, clicked away on the computer as the patients slept. She liked working third shift because it allowed her the opportunity to do her homework. Samantha yearned for the day of graduation. She never worked overtime, and was content about her net pay. She knew she'd be worth a lot more value and money once she wrapped her hand around a degree.

Samantha stopped typing for a second, and moved to the window to see if Adam was still inhaling death. Since Samantha was out of her own squares, she wondered if Adam could spare her one. She looked out the window, and saw Adam sprawled out, hanging off the steps. She turned around, horrified, only to be met by a ski masked man. He placed his plastic gloved hand over her mouth and beckoned her, with his finger over his lip, to be quiet. He said, "*Bitch, you say one word, and you'll die. Cooperate. I know this is a group home and y'all medicate these motherfuckers. Where those pills at?*"

Samantha was petrified, but she wasn't stupid. She pointed at the key near the computer. Luke knew where the key was, but he had to perfect a role. Samantha knew Luke well enough to know his voice so he kept quiet, and followed Dan's instruction. Samantha cried and wept as Dan roped her legs, taped her mouth, and tied her wrists together.

After he placed all the controlled medication in the laundry bag, Dan pointed at her purse. Luke liked Samantha, but she didn't have to come up with one point five million. Luke rummaged through Samantha's purse and found a few hundred dollars. Blind folded, confused, gagged, tied, and scared, she heard the men whisper and was unable to place the voices. She felt one of them move closer, and she stiffened.

"Look shorty, you got nothing to worry about. We need a few more things from you, and we out. Where's the cash y'all use to keep up with this house?" Dan asked as he removed her gag. He knew it was petty cash, but Dan wanted to be as far away from the group home, work lingo as he could. He wanted no fingers pointed at Luke.

Luke looked out the window, and noticed Adam shifting positions on the concrete. Samantha whimpered and trembled. She was so shook that she pointed a finger at another locked box in the closet.

"The key is in the file cabinet next to the bathroom. Please don't hurt me!" Samantha's face was beet red.

After the pair gathered the petty cash, pills, personal cell phones, work cell phones, Adam's Apple computer, and anything valuable with gloves still on, the men successfully made their escape. A client woke up, discovered a panic-stricken Samantha, and freed her from her restraint. A dazed Adam walked up the stairs; he bled profusely from his mouth. Samantha went to the neighbor's house to call the police. A few hours later, the first shift employees walked into a police force when they arrived for duty.

CHAPTER 13

IKE AND ELIZABETH ROMANOV-COLLIN'S mansion was spacious, and guards occupied it. Rottweiler's roamed the perimeter freely. One roamed the inside, well-trained enough not to break anything in the lavish residence. A guard toured the mansion; his shoes click clacked against the Italian marble floor. Equipped with security, cameras, and vicious dogs, no intruder would walk off of the perimeter alive.

Elizabeth cursed, ridiculed, and belittled Luz, the aging Hispanic housekeeper Ike hired over a year ago. Suspended over a toilet by a Hoyer lift, Elizabeth hurled many obscenities as Luz struggled to position her over the toilet. Finally satisfied with her placement, Elizabeth urinated and shitted without shame. Her crude personality had its origins in a past of brutal trauma.

In 1964, during Elizabeth's senior year in high school, she was awarded a full scholarship to Yale, but her smile faded when Elizabeth walked home from school and saw her parents and younger brothers murdered. The blood from her family's headshots littered the apartment floor with a crimson red. She knew her father ripped off a made man, but that was all in her name. Her father wanted his only daughter to escape the world of crime and blue collared employment, and to be self-reliant and money conscious. Elizabeth became an austere woman the second her innocent eyes fell on her dead family. She graduated from Yale, landed a great job, and met Bruno Collins. She never competed for a position because the kingpin, ten years her junior, showered her with swank shelter, a high-end life, and a golden security blanket. Even though she held degrees in Economics and

Mathematics, the lavish lifestyle Bruno provided allowed her to quit her job, and she hadn't worked since. Bruno toured the world. He struck deals, created allies, and he accumulated enemies in the diverse drug trade in the seventies and eighties while Elizabeth raised Ike like he was her own. She never had children, but Elizabeth raised and home-schooled Ike until high school. Elizabeth groomed Ike into a genius, but as Ike got older, Bruno showed Ike a darker side of living. Bruno inflicted harm, tortured, and severed bodies in front of his only son, planting the seed of brutality that would flaw Ike's personality in years to come.

Ike walked smoothly into the massive bathroom. He thumbed through the mail the guard downstairs handed to him. Ike maneuvered four guards in different areas of the mansion, and he stationed an extra guard who spied on the two guards that patrolled the ground level area. Ike and Elizabeth, feared and powerful, were wanted dead by countless enemies. The guard in the camera room never took his eyes from the monitor because he knew better. The previous guard slept soundly at his post, but paid the price with his life.

Elizabeth continued her verbal onslaught in spite of Ike's presence. After Luz wiped her clean and situated Elizabeth in her Hoveround electric wheelchair, Ike remembered Elizabeth being the most beautiful specimen God created. He remembered when Elizabeth thought his eyes were innocent. She used to walk freely around the house naked. Ike's lust for women peaked because of her. Now, in her old age, the Parkinson Disease robbed her of her beauty and body.

Her once long, thick, sandy brown mane had turned into scraggly gray straight hair. Her once toned body dropped into loose folds of skin that was associated with age and her illness. Behind her seemingly sympathetic warm blue eyes hid many layers of evil. Red lipstick covered her thin lips. Bedsores and rashes littered a portion of her body. Bruno's incarceration was the start of the end of her flawless beauty. The turmoil she harbored intensified when she learned of Bruno's murder.

Ike overheard his stepmother deliver another insult to Luz. With a gentle wave of the hand, he relieved Luz of her duties. While Luz exited the bathroom, Ike pulled her to the side and gave her a wad of cash. Luz's hands trembled with anger, and her large brown eyes were red and teary as she reached out for and accepted the cash. Elizabeth rarely talked while being provided services, but today was a different story.

"I do nothing wrong. I just follow instructions." Her English was broken, but audible.

"So what brings this behavior?" Ike asked.

"Ike!"

"She get phone call. Then she start actin' out."

"Come!" Elizabeth blasted again.

Ike prepared to speak again, but Elizabeth interrupted him as she yelled his name again with more urgency. Ike dismissed Luz and thanked her again. He walked through the doorway with his arms folded.

"For heaven's sake mother, what is it? Must you give Luz a hard time? She does a remarkable job despite the language barrier..."

"Your father was murdered this morning," Elizabeth interrupted.

She gave Ike time to absorb it. The speech about Elizabeth's treatment of the housekeeper never left his mouth.

"What?"

"Shall I say it again?"

"Who? What?"

"Lets go to the pool," she said.

Ike dismissed the guards away for privacy. He pulled her from her wheelchair onto the patio furniture. He adjusted his stepmother's body into position.

"He was repeatedly stabbed by an inmate while he slept."

"Mother, he is in a super max prison. How could that be?"

Elizabeth pulled her hair to the side and looked at Ike, her blue eyes cold and vengeful. Her crying and whimpering turned into barely contained anger.

"A hit. It was Maximilian Coffman."

Anger shot through Ike like a bolt of lightening. He stared blankly at the pool while Elizabeth tuned him in on more intricate details of his father's murder. Maximilian Coffman possessed the power to carry out a hit in a super max. He was a former employee of Bruno's who had the heart to cross him. Locked up and out the game, Maximilian had come up, situated himself on top, and remained there since Bruno was bagged and sentenced twenty years ago.

"He bit the hand that fed him, betrayed him, and then murdered him. He must die Ike." She took Ike's hands and held them tightly. "He knows nothing of you as an adult. You know your father always had a solid barrier between his family and his business except when he allowed you to see the demon in him."

Elizabeth saw the expression on Ike's face.

"There is a lot of things you may think I'm not aware of, but that isn't even a slither of significance at this moment."

"Where is he?"

"I don't know, but I do know where he'll be in a few weeks. Just be prepared and ready to go. And remember, what your doing is in our honor. No sidekicks. You do this alone," Elizabeth said.

Nothing else was said. After Ike and Elizabeth schemed some more, they went back inside the comfort of their mansion. The guards resumed their duties. Ike helped Elizabeth with more of her daily routine before he left. He got into his Porsche and jetted off grounds. Halfway down the street, Ike pulled over and began to weep loudly. He clenched his fists in grief and banged the dashboard, stricken by the realization that his dad, the infamous Bruno, was now a memory.

CHAPTER 14

Luke walked through downtown Waterbury. He wore headphones, and was dressed in a Sacred Heart High School uniform. Luke looked sharp. His high fade glistened in the sun. A Jansport backpack draped over one of Luke's shoulders. His thoughts were centered on final exams. The day was hot and humid, and he couldn't wait until school let out for the summer. Luke worked tooth and nail to make his way onto the honor roll, and he couldn't wait until he was able to breath again. Book smart and intelligent, Luke dreamed of attending Tuskegee University. He wanted to study Business Administration. Luke wanted to be married and own a home by the time he was twenty-five. Dreams occupied his genius mind.

Twenty-five minutes later, Luke walked on Cooke Street. The music blared so loudly that he didn't hear anyone honking the horn at him. The driver drove a few yards ahead of Luke to get his attention. Luke recognized the driver, and he made his way to the car.

"Omar, what up?"

"You fam. On your way to the crib?"

"Yeah. I got to study for my trigonometry exam."

Luke couldn't detect the motive in Omar's eyes because of his dark shades. Omar twisted and turned his small dreads while he schemed.

Luke's first instinct told him to keep it moving, but he wouldn't mind the extra cash. Luke was out of tune with the streets, but he sensed that Omar was indirectly enticing him to jump out of the lame life for a second.

"Look man, I got a bill for you if you want it. I need you to handle something for me real quick."

Luke looked at him curiously.

"What do I need to do?"

69

"Bag up some crack."

Luke and Omar pulled up to a ramshackle three-family home on Orange Street. The spring weather drove the flunkies standing around the house out of hibernation. Local misfits were on the street, and they served junkies their slow death. When Luke and Omar stepped out of the car, Steven pulled up behind Omar's car with a menacing look on his face. Luke didn't expect to see his brother at the spot, but there he was. Steve boiled with rage.

"What the fuck are you doing here Luke?"

"I uh, well..."

"Get the fuck in the car!"

Luke was embarrassed, but he followed Steve's command and made his way to the car. When he got in it, Luke rolled down the window and heard Steve's obscenities.

"Nigga, you was about to have my brother bag crack up in this bitch?"

Beads of sweat formed on Omar's brow.

"I didn't think nothing of it dawg. Brandon got locked up, and the shit needs to be moved. We needed a fill-in! Why is you buggin' Steve? Better him than a nigga we don't know."

Steve looked at Omar incredulously before he removed his pistol from his waistband. Luke's eyes expanded to the size of saucers.

"Look motherfucker, this building is hot, and its hours away from being a fucking target and you got my brother up in this shit? Is you fuckin' crazy? If you ever pull some shit like this again, I'm gonna fuckin' kill you!"

Steve pulled Omar away from the car with the gun still in his hand, and Steve shoved him harshly against the same car. Omar considered retaliating, but thought better of it. Steve was strapped, and he was more aggressive by nature than Omar. Instead, Omar remained against the car, his pride snapped in two, and stared at Steven's back as he walked away. Omar stayed in that position until Steve peeled off.

"Luke, let me explain something to you. You my little brother and I love you. I'll be goddamned if I let you tip toe into the game, fuck that. You ain't built for this shit. Niggas like Omar been taught and fed dirt his whole life, so he don't

know any better, but you do. After you graduate from high school, you going to college and that's the end of that."

"My bad Steve, I just didn't think it was a big deal. I didn't think a hundred dollars was bad for bagging."

Steve looked at Luke like his mind fell from his head.

"A hundred fuckin' dollars? That's the problem Luke, you didn't think for a hundred dollars, you almost laid your life on the line 'cause I know for a fact that shit about to be raided. It takes Brandon hours to bag all that shit. You would've been there until tomorrow." Steve drove though Walnut, and en route to the house they were raised in. "I'm coming to tell niggas to close shop, but Omar got you in a hot zone...for a hundred fuckin' dollars. I oughta shoot his ass over that shit."

Steve pulled into their mother's driveway backwards, and he kept the engine running. Steve continued to lecture Luke until his cell phone chimed. The person on the other end confirmed that the cook and bag house got raided while the young street soldiers packed.

Steve looked at his brother and smirked.

"The spot you was going to bag at for a hundred dollars just got knocked...and so did Omar. You would have been included." Steve allowed the news to settle before he went into his pocket. Steve pulled out a wad of hundreds, and peeled off two grand.

"Get out and go study," Steve said. He gripped his brother's hand, and pulled Luke in for a brotherly embrace.

Luke stood at the door, happy as hell and two thousand dollars richer, while Steve drove slowly out of the driveway. Steve stopped the car, and called out to Luke just as he halfway entered the house.

"Do what you supposed to do bro," Steve said, and he coasted down the street.

The exotic weed stirred old memories of Steve's protectiveness. Luke sat alone on the third floor porch. He sulked as he bitterly contemplated the predicament his brother's absence now left with him. Luke wiped his face with his sleeve as he refocused his mind on the present. He had to go downstairs and rejoin Dan and the crack head that owned the building. The cocaine they'd robbed for wasn't going to cook and bag itself. It needed to be moved.

CHAPTER 15

TWO WEEKS AFTER THE group home invasion and other heists, Luke was sprawled out on his own bed. He pondered the conversation he had with his mother an hour ago. Renee became suspicious of Luke. She felt in her gut that something was wrong. The pain in her voice fueled his anger. The criminal lifestyle Luke been forced into made his heart harden, but the sound of his mother expressing her concern and fear bothered him to a point of distraction.

Luke decided to smoke a little weed before he started his day. He lit the blunt, and pulled on it five times before he heard his cell phone vibrate on the dresser. Luke looked at the number, and he didn't recognize it. He figured Dan was calling, and he used a pre-paid phone. When Luke answered the call, he didn't recognize the voice, but it uttered "detective."

"Luke, I'm calling you because I have a few questions to ask you..."

"So ask them." Luke interrupted. He wasn't in any mood to be pressed by a desperate detective.

"Down here at the station," the detective said.

"At the station? What the fuck? About what?"

"Mr. Law, its your choice. Either be here within an hour, or have a warrant out for your arrest. I'm Officer Cavanaugh, and we're located in Southington on Lazy Lane. Make the right choice."

NEXT OF KIN

Detective Cavanaugh was a thin, tall, balding gray man. He wore a long outdated handlebar mustache. Luke never seen him before, but he hated the arrogant, underpaid detective upon first sight.

"Mr. Law, we understand you've worked for the agency a number of years. According to your attendance record, you haven't missed a day in over three years. And as of late, you've been putting in a lot of overtime, working four consecutive overtime shifts in a row. Studies have shown that..."

"Hold it right there. What kind of picture are you trying to paint?" Luke chuckled. "Are you insinuating that I'm tired, burned out, and would be capable of murdering a patient where I work at?"

The detective's face turned beet red with embarrassment; he thought Luke was a dumb ass. Detective Cavanaugh knew that his suspect was going to be a problem.

"Mr. Law, I..."

"Nah, hold up. You threaten me to come down here and talk, so lets talk. How many suspects are white? Probably none. His redneck family don't like or respect black people so we automatic suspects. I bet you that highly assaultive, high functioning white motherfucker didn't get questioned."

"Let's not get overly defensive here Luke. I'm following protocol. The entire staff is being questioned so save the race card."

"Save this entire investigation."

Detective Cavanaugh glared at Luke coldly. "Ok wise ass, I'm not in the mood so cut your Black Panther horse shit."

"This conversation is done. My attorney isn't present, and you have no reason to arrest me." Luke got up. The detective was pissed because Luke was right. He had no reason to be there besides questioning. Detective Cavanaugh wasn't going to let Luke walk away without putting something in his head.

"There has been a burglary and robbery at the agency. We have our eyes and ears open," Detective Cavanaugh said nonchalantly.

The detective's words hit Luke's head like a pillowcase filled with rocks. Since Luke was partially out the door when the detective made his statement, Luke kept his motion. A good detective could read a bold faced lie on a suspect. Instead of turning around, and feeding into the statement, Luke walked out of the police station with something new to worry about.

Bud Cook, a young, tall lanky white dude with wispy hair, stood amongst his friends and smoked cigarettes and drank *Natural Ice,* the official beer of the house party. The crowd was thick, and partygoers flanked much of the space in the first floor apartment.

"Jesus Christ dude, she is fucking shit faced," Bud said jokingly while he watched a chubby long hair woman sleep and drunk on the floor, her chin touching her large chest.

"So why don't you lay your pipe game on her," a short, skinny red head man with bad acne said..

"That's too much weight for my small cock. I like 'em skinny," Bud laughed. "Besides, I'd rather fuck your grandmother than to have all that extra meat on my rod."

Red head bent over in laughter. He opened his mouth to retaliate, but Julius, an overweight man the same age as Bud, and the only black man in the circle, chimed in before him.

"Bud, you better be glad that somebody would be willing to give your ugly ass some pussy."

"Oh yeah? You need to go over there and whip out your big Kunte Kinte cock. You colored people love big white chicks," Bud fired back.

Everyone laughed, including Julius. While they continued to rank and shoot shit, Bud spotted a woman that was out of his league. She stared in his direction. Bud prayed to the gods that he was the one she was interested in. Everyone else in the small circle noticed her leer as well.

"She must see something here she likes, and it's me. Julius, you're a fat fuck, and Frank, you're the worst looking guy in here," Bud said convincingly.

"Fuck you Bud," Julius and Red head said in unison.

Bud ignored them, and walked slowly to the beautiful specimen. When he approached and greeted her, Bud's friends looked on with astonishment. They watched Bud for the next ten minutes in action.

NEXT OF KIN

He talked and hugged her before the pair disappeared out the backdoor. Bud's friends watched on with envy.

Bud and Daphney talked for the next hour about honor and commitment. Bud didn't want the night to end, especially after she fondled his dick. They shared a deep kiss. Bud managed to unsnap her bra, and get a handful. He lifted her shirt, and began to suck her breasts, but she stopped him.

"Bud, wait, I like you and all, but I think we are moving way too fast," she said.

Disappointment lined on his face, but Bud complied. Besides, he wanted her on a king sized bed instead of the backseat of his late model Ford. Bud's dick was so hard that he nearly ejaculated. Bud didn't want to fuck it up with Daphney; he saw a bright future with her.

"I so understand and I'm sorry. Please forgive me."

Daphney smiled and touched his face.

"Its ok. It takes two you know. I never felt this way about any guy. Where have you been all my life?"

Bud smiled and revealed crooked teeth.

"I don't know Daphney, but I'm here now. I have a question for you. Where do we go from here?"

"Do you believe in love at first sight?"

"Yes Daphney, I do."

Daphney picked a piece of lint from her shirt. "So there's your answer."

"Are you serious? So we're boyfriend and girlfriend?"

"Yes and yes!" She gave Bud a peck on his cheek.

Bud and Daphney talked about commitment. Bud's work schedule didn't allow him any room for the rest of the week, but he figured he'd squeeze in a little time.

After Bud hit his bed after a long night of drinks, drugs, and love, Bud jerked off as he visualized Daphney's slanted crystal blue eyes, stunning smile, and her tits. After he shot a load on an old t-shirt, Bud slept soundly throughout the night.

CHAPTER 16

THE TURQUOISE WATER IN the Tobago Cays exposed the schools of exotic fish that swam alongside the boat. Fifty-two-year-old Maximilian Coffman wasn't impressed, but he enjoyed his yacht. Max puffed moderately on his cigar. He enjoyed his wealth and swank aura. His *Moss Liplow* shades covered half his aging face, and they concealed the lust in his eyes. Before him was an exotic and petite woman from the Dominican Republic with her long, curly, dark brown hair draped over her shoulders. Max was in the mood for fun. His dick was hard, and he wouldn't mind spending money to keep her around for the weekend. Max left Nancy, his wife of twenty-five years, in Palm Island. She complained of a headache and turned in early. Max was fully charged, and was ready to get into something. He lingered around the resort long enough to reel in the bronzed beauty. Smelling money, she kept Max company.

Max had spent the last few days snorkeling, mingling with locals, and swimming with sea turtles. He ate lobster, drank, and humped the finest pussy while his wife napped. Max wined, dined, courted, and enjoyed his wife during their time together, but new pussy was always one of his strongest vices.

Max's hired captain rode him and his companion between Petit Bateau and Petit Rameau. International tourists crowded the Caribbean, and flooded it with noise. A large group of college kids drank beer and dived. All the activities were trivial to Max. He'd been there and done that. Graffiti that belonged to him was stained on rocks. Max smoked and snorted drugs, humped whore pussy, and experienced paradise that dated back to the seventies. He plunged into the dope game, became a great follower, enforced the rules of the trade, betrayed allies when necessary, and stayed at the top.

The yacht was equipped with luxury and high-end amnesties. A plush carpeted spiral staircase led to the upper level. Expensive furniture ordered from other countries surrounded the small quarters that resembled a five-star suite. Max and his guest cuddled, giggled, and flirted. He was relaxed in his khaki shorts and multi-colored buttoned down shirt that exposed a chunk of hair on his chest. Max head was boxed shaped. He was average height, and had a protruding gut from being comfortable. Max wore a light salt and pepper beard, and his graying hair was receded.

The top to the Dominican woman's two-piece bathing suit was small. Half of her light brown areola stuck out of her top. Max's erection rose to the occasion. He casually removed his shades, and anticipated a fuck fest. Buzzed from the Louis the thirteenth, Max made moves on her. He fondled her breasts, and stroked her nipples. His salt and pepper whiskers grazed her skin. Max panted with overwhelming pleasure as he struggled to control himself. He came up for air, and saw the captain walk past the room. Max found it odd, but didn't think anything of it, or of his current location in the ocean. When he walked by the second time, the goddess noticed, but Max discarded all shame and continued to indulge. The woman sensed the captain lingering around the door, and she wanted Max to chill for the moment. Max settled himself after he read her body language. He made a mental note to check his employee when they reached land.

"So, what education you got to show for all of this?" she asked. Her English was a little broken, but crisp.

"My own education. Self-made one zero one. And believe me, a book didn't put me here. Everything I learned was hands-on. I never made a short cut. Quick and easy equals doom."

"What is it that you do Mr. Reilly?" Max never revealed his real name to random women. A mistake like that could ruin him.

Max relit his cigar, and blew out a series of smoke rings while he pondered the question.

"Its not what I do, its how I do it. I don't do much. I have power. I tell people to do everything," Max said arrogantly.

"Drug dealer? Kingpin?"

Max chuckled.

"Very powerful and successful businessman."

"Your wife?"

"You're not a decoy from *Cheaters*, are ya?"

"Successful businessmen have insecure wife."

The split second Max attempted to utter a response, he looked out the window and noticed nothing but open water, not a tourist in sight.

"Michael, is this some kind of shortcut? Jamesby is nowhere near us! What the fuck?"

"Please Mr. Reilly, I'm sure he know direction."

The captain opened the door to the suite, and walked gingerly down the staircase before he collapsed to his death. The captain's body never made it to the lower level. Blood poured from the fresh wounds on the captain's neck and his mouth. The woman screamed. Max kept his lips pursed and remained calm. He shuffled around a moment before finding the lock box that held his gun and opened it. After he retrieved and stashed it, another man that carried a scabbard on his side, and wore a fisherman's hat walked down the stairs slowly in tow, whistling a tune.

"I'm afraid you can't be here on the premises. Get off the boat," the man ordered the woman.

"But I no swim." The woman cried and whimpered. She was horrified, and at the wrong place at the wrong time. Max was not a stranger to death around him. He kept his eyes on the intruder, and he fished for ideas of escape or murder.

The man smiled wickedly. "I'm pretty sure stiffs can float."

When the woman opened her mouth to speak, the assassin flung a folding knife that landed squarely in the middle of her gullet. Blood spilled from her neck as she flopped into the arms of a man she met two hours ago. Max moved her harshly to the side while she bled and gagged, and he continued to pull on his cigar as he tried to mentally set up a defense and offense against a man that was out for his blood. The more Max stared at the man, the more it became clear.

"Mr. Coffman."

Max smiled.

NEXT OF KIN

"Ike, you were just a boy the last time I saw you. I thought I was looking at Bruno's ghost, but I don't believe in them. I always thought you were going to be a fag."

"I'm quite impressed by your bravery and your steel machismo I must say, but I'm overtly displeased by my father's murder. You're over your expiration date."

"Is that right? Your father betrayed my brother by killing him."

"My father never tolerated disloyalty and piracy. Your brother was indigent when he got on his hands and knees and begged my father to lift him onto his feet, just like yourself. He groomed you two goons from petty thieves to kings of your environment. And then you sided with the enemy when he went to trial. While your brother was being a tattletale, you sided with the adversary while he was held captive and unable to defend himself...and you got him slain."

"Spare me the Shakespeare Othello. Your father humiliated, spilled blood, pissed, and shitted on my family for years. My brother and I tried to walk away quietly and respectfully, but he wouldn't let us. So we became proactive. Bruno was inactive so I took it out on him. Why not? He slaughtered our lives and I slaughtered his. He killed a few of mine; I took him directly. Its all game Ike and you know it," Max said. He rose to the occasion, and drew his weapon. Ike smirked and knew Max wasn't going to go quietly.

The men faced off from a distance. Max pulled the trigger, but no shot was fired. He pulled the trigger several more times before he realized that it wasn't a hang fire; the gun was unloaded.

"Missing these?" Ike smirked and spilled the bullets on the floor.

Max hurled the gun at him, and missed badly. He saw no other option, and Max closed a little distance before he tossed his cigar at him, hoping the ember of it would blind Ike, and allow Max enough time to turn the tables, but Ike anticipated and dodged it. Max stepped back. Ike stood his ground casually. Beads of sweat dripped off Max's face as his mind scrambled. Ike reached into his scabbard, and displayed the handle of a sword. Max saw one weapon and one opportunity. Max charged at Ike full speed to stop him from drawing the sword, but Ike kept both butterfly swords in the same scabbard. Ike gave him the illusion of having one sword, while one was hidden from Max's sight. When Ike dual wielded them, the first one pierced

79

Max's heart. After Max felt the puncture, Ike swung the second sword, and turned Max into a headless corpse. Max's head rolled near the couch. Blood spurted out of the stomp of Max's neck before his body dropped to the floor. Ike picked up Max's head, and stuffed it into the thin knapsack he carried along with his tools of death. Ike whistled another slow, eerie tune before making his way to the driver's seat of the yacht. He sailed it deeper into the Caribbean to rid the bodies.

CHAPTER 17

UKE OPENED THE DOOR to the hotel room at Foxwoods Casino with Zora in tow. Nervous anticipation, excitement, and strong curiosity had been brewing since the start of their date at Hubbard Park in Meriden, CT. They walked a few hiking trails before they drove to *Castle Craig*. After walking up the metal interior, Luke talked about the origin of the castle before taking the stairs to the observation deck. Zora gasped at the expansive view of greater Meriden, New Haven, the Long Island Sound, and the Hartford skyline before she compared it to New York's infamous skyline. When they left the park, they conversed over breakfast and coffee at Dunkin Donuts, and then decided on the casino to go gambling. Zora wanted to pick Luke's brain and have fun. Luke planned the casino jump-off because he wanted to turn the five thousand dollars in his pocket into five digits. The life or death circumstance forced his mind into an elite state of money consciousness. Luke hadn't played a hand in Texas Hold'em in two years, but his skill level was high. And despite the risk, Luke was strapped with a three eighty Kel Tec. The gun was compact, and easy access in case Toby wanted to appear and draw blood from him and his companion. Luke saw Toby six times since his first date with Zora. But tonight proved to be danger-free as Luke spent hours on poker while Zora played the slots, and there was still no sign of the assassin.

As the night trudged on, Luke won seven hundred dollars; it was a small amount of money, but it was better than nothing. Zora won a hundred on the slots, and was high with joy. Luke and Zora ate, drank, and called it a night. It was Zora's idea to get a hotel room since they were too touched by the liquor they'd consumed throughout the day.

Luke was taken back by the request, but he wasn't going to argue it. Moments of subtle embraces transpired throughout the date. They strolled through the casino with their arms draped around one another. Their conversations were deep and flirtatious, but Luke thought they were going to end their night with a kiss in front of her residence, and leave it at that. But Zora had something else in mind.

Luke and Zora got situated in the luxurious room. Luke went into the bathroom after she used it. After he washed up, butterflies surfaced in the pit of his stomach. When he came out of the bathroom, Luke discovered that darkness hid everything out of sight. He made his way to the bed, and got into it. Luke placed his arms behind his head, his dick rock solid, and wrestled with the urge to touch her. Taking a chance, Luke wrapped his arm around her. Naked, she waited for Luke's touch. Zora snaked her arm around his neck, and pulled Luke's head to the nape of her neck. Luke licked softly across it. She pressed against him, and reached behind for his penis. Zora pulled it out his boxers, and placed Luke's penis between her legs. She writhed in passion and lust. Sensual moans escaped Zora's mouth when Luke cuffed her breasts. She rolled off her side and unto her back. Luke got on his knees, and moved between her thighs. He took a second to marvel at her beautiful, tight body before he kissed her. Their foreplay had the right mixture of stop and go. They tasted, sucked, and tested boundaries. Luke pulled her arms over her head. He held both her wrists with one hand. He kissed, sucked her nipples, and rubbed his bare tool on her treasure. Zora wanted to feel him. She couldn't tolerate any more foreplay. Luke teased her when he rubbed his shaft on the entrance to her pussy, but she shifted downward. She dared him to put it in. Zora had a hunch Luke didn't have protection, and neither did she, but the temptation was too strong for them. Luke entered, pumped slowly, and increased his speed. Zora's moans stretched, and were drawn out with desire. Her legs squeezed his waist as she met every one of his deep strokes.

On the brink of Luke's climax, Luke pulled out abruptly. He didn't want the session to end prematurely, but she understood. During the intermission, he sucked, licked, and chewed her body. Zora's large, dark brown, silver dollar areolas turned him on, and they were sensitive. She rubbed Luke's dick across her nipples before taking him in her mouth. They shifted to a sixty-nine. Luke licked her anus while he two finger fucked her. After several positions and foreplay engagements, Zora turned her back to him, and he entered with one of her legs between his, and the other one up in the air. She lay half-turned on her side, his penis making her thrust forward, her mouth opened and eyes half-slit. Luke pounded her. Animal noises oozed out of her mouth when she exploded on his shaft. Zora's nails drilled into Luke's skin while she jerked from her climax. Luke stroked some more before he ejaculated in her. They remained in that position for a while, their chemistry too powerful and potent to separate.

Zora had a horrid look on his face. "You're telling me someone is trying to kill you?"

Luke pulled on his Black and Mild. "That's exactly what I told you Zora."

Luke told her everything. He wanted to be free of the restraint of a lie. He liked her, and felt Zora deserved the truth. He didn't like the blank look on her face, but he felt good for telling her.

Luke sighed. "Zora, I don't want you in my shit."

"You mean your brother's shit."

"You know what I mean."

Zora had her head down, sadden by Luke's reality. "I don't know Luke. I liked you the first day I met you and felt the connection, but I have a lot to live for, and don't want to die carelessly."

"That's why we are better off not seeing each other. Not yet. At least until everything is clear."

The comforter slipped under Zora's breasts while she tied her hair into place. He dreaded the conversation, but couldn't keep his eyes off her set. The pair slipped back under the covers, and received another dose of uncertainty. They wanted one another, but they knew the circumstances were grave. Zora found it hard to believe someone wanted her new interest dead, but why would he lie?

"Its win or die. And I don't plan on dying anytime soon," Luke said.

Luke and Zora made love three more times before sunrise. On the way home, silence filled the rental car. Zora was upset about Luke's revelation, but on the other hand, she wanted him badly. Luke felt he'd never hear from her again, and as much as it hurt him, he had to admit he couldn't blame her if Zora left him. At least then she would be alive.

CHAPTER 18

BUD DROVE THE ARMORED truck slowly through light traffic in Naugatuck near Rubber Ave. His partner, Gary Windham, a short, pudgy, black sleek haired guard in his early thirties, spoke obsessively about his interest in guns. Bud barely listened. Daphney rented space in his mind. Bud hoped she'd be on time. He looked at his smartphone, and expected it to chime any second. Daphney called him fifteen minutes ago, but he wanted to be sure he wasn't in a dream. Bud was wide open, and couldn't wait to lay his eyes on her again. Daphney's divine beauty woke him up at night with a hard-on. He'd text her in moving traffic, and he used his legs to steer the wheel. The memories of their first encounter at the party distracted Bud from obligations. He daydreamed of fucking her raw. He masturbated twice a day. Bud told all his friends and family he had a girlfriend. His friends told him to get a grip. They knew he never had a chance encounter with her besides the party. Bud was in love.

"Bud, what the fuck? The light is green. You've been looking at your phone. Christ man, she said she'd be there. Relax."

"Dude, you're telling *me* to relax? Every time your girlfriend comes around, I walk on fuckin' eggshells. My words are limited at your shack. But you're telling me to relax. You're such a dick."

Gary lit a Marlboro Light with his beefy hands. Bud made a right and pulled into an empty lot, and drove all the way to the back to avoid being seen. The men could hear the traffic on Route 8 from where they parked, as the highway was right behind them.

"Looking at your phone and driving a loaded armored truck doesn't go hand to hand Bud, and neither does being in a vacant lot sitting in an armored truck at six-forty-five in the morning. There are millions of dollars in this puppy," Gary said.

"Are you serious? You're talking this ethic shit, and you used an armored truck to move furniture," Bud shot back.

"That was six years ago asshole."

"Doesn't matter. If I weren't working with you, you'd still make sure the surveillance is turned off. Besides, I'm meeting my girlfriend for ten minutes, not moving a couch or table set."

Gary chuckled. "Your girlfriend, huh? How long you known her? Seventy two hours?"

"Two weeks to be exact. Don't throw dirt on *my* happiness because you're stuck with a fat baby mother and her own three kids."

"Fuck you Bud. A lot of it is water retention. What are you, like twenty-six and only had sex twice? Playgirl isn't knocking on your door either."

Bud and Gary laughed in unison because there was truth to it. The men had known each other for eight years. They launched crude jokes at each other, but nothing was ever taken personally. Harm or cruel intent never lingered behind their words.

Bud's phone stopped Gary's statement. Bud's excitement caused him to fumble for the phone and hit the wrong button, but the connection remained intact.

"Five minutes?" Bud glanced at his watch and had over twenty minutes to kill with Daphney.

"Ok, love you too. Bye."

Gary cracked a smile, shook his head, and kept his opinion to himself.

"We got a little time, but remember, we were dispatched to the bank an hour ago, and the bank is right up the road. We don't need anyone associated with this company fucking us with an unauthorized stop," Gary said.

"I don't think those six figure fucks would be up this early, but I hear ya."

Gary started across the parking lot en route to Dunkin' Donuts. He chuckled, and he thought of Bud's quick love connection. Gary couldn't believe Bud claimed her as his girlfriend. *He's making himself look stupid.* Gary picked up his pace, and hoped the line wasn't long so he could get their usual quickly. He wondered what Bud's new girlfriend looked like, or if she had a friend. Gary figured he could use some good, new pussy in his life. He did, however, find it strange that Bud and his new interest only found time for one another an hour after sunrise. And then it hit him. Gary turned around and saw Bud leaning on the truck smoking a cigarette, and checking his phone. Ignoring his first instinct, Gary continued his way to get the fuel to jumpstart the day. On his way back, he dropped breakfast, pulled out his Glock 19, and moved hastily towards the truck. Bud's life was in danger.

Bud's heart rate reached its peak. Daphney said she'd be there in five minutes. Seven minutes vanished. He called her back five times, but her phone was off. Bud theorized that she was lost, but he kicked that hypothesis out the door. Daphney picked the place to meet. The second Bud's thumb touched his phone, an old Chevy Malibu loaded with three masked goons screeched to a halt alongside the armored truck. One of them drew his weapon when Bud dropped the phone and reached for his waist.

"Put them hands were I can see them. You know what this is. Cooperate or die," gunman number one said evenly. "Lets not turn this into a blood bath. Give him the key to the back."

Bud didn't have to think twice. He handed gunman number two the key to the treasure chest. Bud scanned for his partner. He wished to God he could alert Daphney, but he was being held at gunpoint.

"Turn around and face the truck."

The gunman took his weapon, snapped a set of handcuffs on Bud, and shoved him violently to the ground. Bud heard the duo in the back of the truck on the brink of stealing millions. They transported trays of cash to the trunk of the Chevy Malibu without dialogue, and with brisk efficiency. The raucous in the truck ceased after Gary fired two shots from two hundred feet. Dan's body fell from the truck to the pavement. Rosa's body produced the second thud inside the truck. Brain matter, cranium, pus, and blood oozed out of the gaping hole of Dan's ski mask. Dan never knew what hit him. Blood pooled around his head. Luke couldn't see the shooter, but he saw his best friend's corpse. He lifted Bud off the ground, and trained his gun on him. Luke didn't have time to access the situation, but he had a hostage.

"Drop your weapon!" Gary yelled from behind the truck.

"You drop *your* weapon, or I'll put a fuckin' hole in your partner's head!"

Gary peeked around the armor truck, and didn't see Bud or the gunman. The shots Gary fired were deafeningly loud. He figured someone had heard them and called the police. Gary's body was drenched with perspiration as he positioned his back on the truck. He held his smoking gun with two hands. He stared at one of the bodies he cut down. He wanted to kneel and look underneath the truck to see if he could spot the gunman's legs, but didn't want to get ambushed with bullets.

After a few minutes of silence, Gary raised his weapon, but lowered it when he saw Bud make his way around the truck wearing handcuffs.

"Dude, he's gone."

"Where the fuck did he go?" Gary looked around. He hoped the gunman wasn't setting a trap.

"I don't fucking know. He had me face the truck when I was on the ground while he still had his gun on me. He made me count to one hundred slowly. I did, turned around, and he was gone. He's more than likely on the highway."

Gary sighed and regained his composure, but kept his gun drawn. Still handcuffed, Bud followed Gary to the first body. Gary pulled the mask off it, but neither of them recognized the young black male. They stepped onto the truck, and approached the second stiff. Gary pulled off the ski mask. It was a petite, brunette woman with crystal blue eyes shifted upwards from the bullet lodged in her Parietal lobe. Bud thought it was a nightmare, but reality came in the form of a corpse. Bud became nauseous and vomited. Gary remembered Bud's description of Daphney. An incredulous look formed on his face before he turned away from the body.

"Please tell me this isn't who I think it is."

The pathetic look on Bud's face gave Gary his answer.

"Dude, she fuckin' set us up! Jesus Christ Bud, how can you be so stupid?"

Bud shook his head, and wiped the vomit from the corners of his mouth. He felt overwhelmed, sick, and dumb.

NEXT OF KIN

"I fucked up big time man. I'll take the total blame," Bud said. He put his head in his arms.

Gary blew out a breath, lit a cigarette, and started orchestrating a plan. The robbery and the killings were due to Bud's stupidity, but Gary wasn't going to let his partner go out by himself. They heard the faint sounds of sirens. By the time the fuzz arrived, the men had a story, but Gary would have to answer for the bodies he put down.

CHAPTER 19

DIRTY, SWEATY, HOT, HYSTERICAL, and paranoid, Luke rushed into his unkempt apartment after fourteen hours running from the botched robbery. Luke endured forces of nature by walking through the woods alongside Route 8 in the rainstorm after Dan and Rosa's deaths. Traumatic memories of Dan's brain matter and Rosa's blood flashed violently in Luke's mind. Regret clouded his aura. Fear about being seen, reported, and captured loomed in his head. Luke sat on his couch, drove his nails into his scalp, flared his nostrils, whispered obscenities, and gritted his teeth to ease the unwanted noise in his head. He tapped his foot repeatedly on the floor. Luke didn't know what to do.

After an hour, Luke settled himself, turned on his personal cell phone, and destroyed the prepaid phone he'd only used to discuss capers with Dan. Luke placed the debris of the phone, the black ski mask, and the shoes he wore at the crime scene into a black garbage bag with his gloves still on. Luke showered, changed clothes, and turned on the television. It was 10:59pm, just in time for the eleven o'clock news. After he watched the segment on the attempted heist, Luke felt at ease. The reporter interviewed the guard who he held hostage. The skinny guard couldn't provide a description other then a ski-masked gunman that wore all black. Nothing was captured on video because the surveillance equipment was conveniently cut off. Luke was thankful the guards couldn't note what direction he ran. His fear ignited again after he thought of the money he could've given to Ike that remained untouched. Luke had fifty thousand dollars stashed, but it was nowhere near one point five million. He jumped when his cell phone chimed. Luke didn't recognize the number so he let it go to voicemail. His phone chimed again. It was the same number. Curiosity drove Luke to answer the call.

"Hello?"

"Luke?"

"Who's this?" Luke asked.

"This is Rhonda. You have a minute?" She seemed troubled and off-balanced, but it was natural when death struck home. Rhonda was the mother of Dan's three children.

"Hold on one second." Luke wondered if she was going to question him about the third person in the hold-up. Luke regretted he picked up the phone. He braced himself to be probed, but he planned fast.

"Rhonda, I'm fucked up right now over this shit. I haven't been out of my bed since I heard. I'm sorry Rhonda," Luke said with sincerity. It was hard for him to lie to her, but everyone knew the third man of the attempted heist as a ski masked man who wore all black. The further Luke removed himself from Dan, the better off he would be. He was hurt, grief stricken, and traumatized by Dan's death, but had to mask his feelings as best as he could.

Luke engaged in small talk about being there for the family until Rhonda got to the reason why she called.

"Luke, I know this is hard, and we're weak at the moment, but there is something I need to know."

Luke felt the need to take a shit. Rhonda's tone was eerie and suspect.

"What's that?"

"The truth Luke."

"What truth are you talking about?"

"The white bitch he was killed with."

"Huh?"

"Luke, don't play stupid. Dan is gone now so it doesn't make a difference. How long have they been messing around? Be honest."

"Look Rhonda, with all due respect, how is that even relevant? What will change if I had the answer to your question?" Luke didn't like where the conversation was headed.

"Its relevant to me, especially after finding out Dan and that *bitch* were having a baby. Dan never told you that? He never told you she was three months pregnant? You're his *best* friend!"

Luke was stunned, but curious to how she knew about the baby.

"How did you know she was pregnant?"

Rhonda said, "His cellphone."

Luke was happy they talked primarily on prepaid phones. Dan and Rosa dismantled their phones after Rosa spoke to the guard for the last time before everything went down. Luke had to get Rhonda off the jack. He literally had life and death to think about.

"Rhonda, I'm hurting bad right now, and for the record, no, I didn't know the chick was more than Dan's crime partner. The first time I seen her was on the news. Now if you don't mind, I would like to grieve for my homeboy in peace."

Rhonda hung up on him. Luke let it ride because she was hurt, and she didn't have a tight grip on her emotions. He empathized with her. The only man she'd slept and had children with was dead, and Rhonda felt the harsh sting of betrayal.

Missed calls and text messages from Luke's mother and Zora flooded his cell phone. An incoming call from Zora chimed and vibrated in his hand, but Luke sent the call to voicemail. He didn't have time to offer anything to her despite his feelings for her. Luke was dangerous, and he didn't want anyone around him.

The sound of two bullets from a Glock echoed in Luke's head. Dan's body, the sound of the thump Rosa created in the armor truck when she landed to her sudden death, Luke's kidnapping, Talisha's rendezvouses, the bodies Ike exposed him to, and the mysterious circumstances that surrounded Steven's death circulated in his brain while Luke packed and thought about his next move.

CHAPTER 20

LUKE COUNTED THE MONEY from the rip and run he did in Hartford. Dan wasn't there to guide him, but he'd come off with a decent sized grip. Two weeks had passed since Dan's funeral. Luke's mind was guilt-ridden and murky, and Luke couldn't shake the image of his friend's brains that spilled on the pavement. His thoughts then shifted to the tragic memory of the funeral proceedings. Family and friends wept, Dan's mother screamed in agony, and Rhonda shot daggers at him whenever her attention wasn't on Dan's body. Dan was Rhonda's meal ticket to the fine living that only crime could finance. Although there was no doubt Rhonda was heartbroken, and would grieve for a long period of time, Luke would bet his last dollar that she also carried anger into the Lord's house. And it was directed at the stiff. The only love of her life had stepped out of their common-law union, and impregnated a white chick.

While Luke and the rest of the pallbearers carried Dan's gray casket to his plot in New Pine Grove, plain clothed policemen who wore shades stood in the distance. Luke knew they would be there. If he decided to skip the funeral, a suspicious detective would have made a connection. Hiding in plain sight was ideal, but the thought of prison scared Luke more than death.

Luke shook his head to clear his thoughts and jolt himself back into the present. He continued to store his money. As soon as Luke placed the last stack of cash in his lock box and tucked it away, Talisha barged into the room, and she held his phone.

"Who the fuck is Zora?!"

Under normal circumstances, Luke would have disregarded her, but his current state of mind was dark. Luke looked at her with a snarl on his face she'd never seen. He risked his life everyday to keep himself and the family alive, and Zora walked in with her bullshit. Luke kept her in the dark because she would never understand the seriousness of the situation. However, Luke knew he shouldn't had left his phone in her presence.

"If you really want to know, she is my new interest, and before you ask, yeah, I fucked her, and I have plans to keep fucking her."

Talisha's eyes narrowed to slits. She squeezed his phone like she was on the verge of breaking it.

"Motherfucker, I'm home raising our child and you fuck another bitch?"

Luke lost the scowl on his face and replaced it with a smirk. The bitch had a lot of nerve.

"Me and my mom is raising him while you're out having your threesomes. Do you think I'm *that* stupid? This relationship was on the rocks, but it died a sudden death when I saw cum stains on your thighs."

The truth about her rendezvous was confirmed when she hurled his cell phone at him. The phone missed him as Luke dodged it; he got up, rushed her, and slammed her back against the wall. Talisha struggled with her back against it, but Luke was too angry and strong. His hand was wrapped around her neck. Talisha's deceit, coupled with the horrific traumas that had come into his life since Ike entered it, danced in his mind while Luke choked her. She couldn't breathe. Baron's crying snapped Luke out of murder mode, and it brought him back to reality. When he let her go, Talisha collapsed to the floor. She coughed, weeped, gasped, and trained her cold, vindictive eyes on Luke's back as he walked out the door.

Luke drove around shameful of what he did to Talisha. He'd never attacked a woman, and knew he lost control of himself. He pulled up in front of the three-family home, turned the car off and sulked. He had to get it together. Talisha may be grimy and trifling, but she was a woman, and the mother of his only child. When Luke stepped out of his crasher, a police cruiser pulled up slowly behind it. He knew he'd be waking up his mother to bail him out of jail.

An hour and a half later, Luke's mother bailed him out of jail. Renee criticized and bashed Luke from the time she picked him up from the station until they reached Luke's apartment. A police officer escorted them inside in case Talisha was home. Talisha rudely dropped Baron off at his mother's house a half hour before Renee picked Luke up. Renee was outside. She waited for Luke to finish packing Baron's overnight bag.Despite the shit Luke talked about Wil, he was thankful Wil agreed to watch Baron while Renee got him out of the slammer. Toby was more than likely around the area so he needed to be quick. Talisha's clothes were gone, but he was far from distraught. When Luke couldn't find the lock box he kept his stash in, he fucking flipped.

CHAPTER 21

LUKE PROWLED THE NORTH end section of Waterbury for a week. He couldn't find Talisha. Luke was so pissed that he created a visual of her head being blown off by a bullet. Anger swarmed through his body. Broken furniture was scattered throughout the apartment. Luke paced, screamed, and broke shit. He spent day and night in his car looking for her. Luke called everyone he knew associated with her. He had no reservations about calling night or day. Talisha's few friends and sister figured he was pussy whipped and in stalker mode, but he could care less about her pussy; Luke wanted his money. The thought of his family's life in Talisha's hands made him grit his teeth with rage. Dan's death loomed on the other side of his mind. Guilt and regret kept him from good hygiene. Luke was sweaty, funky, and dangerous. He was no longer a passive, law-abiding, tax-paying citizen. Luke was now a dark and angry marked man trying to pay back a king's ransom.

Small droplets of rain fell from the night sky as he slowed his car to a crawl in front of Pacos. The club was packed. Hustlers and goons loomed around the entrance. *Blackheart Adonis* was in town. His battled-filled voice was heard on the street as he lyrically cut down an adversary. Luke put the hood of his windbreaker on after he got out of the car. He nodded at familiar faces while he moved through the patrons.

After Luke got pat down, he entered the club. The club's patrons were packed around the two lyrical combatants. Blackheart ripped his nemesis so hard that the crowd roared while Luke's eyes made moves throughout the club. He couldn't spot her. Luke wondered through a maze of bodies, and he boiled with hatred. The second he decided to leave, Luke spotted Shameka, Talisha's best friend. She was with her dude, but Luke didn't give a fuck. Shameka was going to cough up some information, even if Luke had to beat it out of her.

Luke tailed the pair until they reached the Marriott in Southington. He parked seven spaces from the couple, got out of the car, and walked casually in their direction with a grip on his gun. Luke figured they were the ones who Talisha had threesomes with, but he didn't care and wasn't gonna ask. A pudgy, dark-skinned man exited the car followed by Shameka. Luke closed in on them.

"Shameka, I need to holla at you in private," Luke said. He ignored her round, corn rowed, dark-skinned counter-part. Feeling the need to tap into his machismo, the dude stepped forward.

"Whoa, whoa. Who the fuck are you?" the dude asked.

Shameka placed her hand on her hip, and looked at Luke like he crawled from underneath a rock. She was short, fat, light-skinned, weaved, and wore a pound of make up on her face.

"First of all, I *know* you didn't follow us up here, and for your information, I don't speak to cowards who put their hands on women," Shameka said with attitude. She felt protected because her homeboy was with her.

"This the nigga that fucked up your homegirl?" the man asked like he was going to do something.

Shameka said, "Yup."

Luke looked at the dude incredulously and held a half smirk, but kept quiet as Luke sized pudgy up.

"And this unemployed, broke ass nigga calls himself a man," Shameka added.

"Yo homie, kick rocks before..."

That was as far as pudgy got before Luke swung the Beretta, and caught the shit talker on the side of his jaw. Luke swore he heard a crack. Pudgy hit the ground, held his shattered jaw with both hands, and squirmed around from the pain. Shameka was stunned. She took Luke as a stalker, womanizer, and coward based on one side of a story, but the deadliness she saw in Luke's eyes was alien.

Luke turned to face Shameka. "Now I'm going to ask you again. Can we talk?"

She nodded out of fear. She knew Luke would become hip to their "threesome meetings," and hoped he wasn't in a homicidal state of mind.

"Ye...yeah, but if it is about the threesome, I'm sorry Luke, but please put the gun away before you make a mistake."

Luke took it off safety, kicked the dude violently in his ribs, grabbed Shameka by her shirt, and planted the barrel of the gun against her temple. Urine trickled down her legs. Luke dragged her out of plain view.

"Bitch, I really don't got time to play games! I don't give a fuck about no threesome! Now tell me where the fuck she is!"

Talisha was one of her best friends, but she would be damned if she died over her bullshit. If Luke wasn't pissed about the threesome, why was he acting out of character? She acted as *hood* as Talisha, but she knew her friend as a fire starter. Shameka looked at her "sometimes" lover clutching his jaw, and grunting from the pavement. The strength in Luke's grip, tone, and nature convinced her Talisha might have gone overboard, but whatever it was, Shameka wanted no part of it. She thought Luke was a lame, and he was, but Shameka was oblivious to his ordeal, and Luke intended to keep it that way.

"Ok. I just need to get my phone out of..."

Luke snatched her purse, rummaged through it, and pulled out her IPhone. Shameka told Luke the password, and where to find the location in Maryland where Talisha was staying. Once Luke got what he needed, he bookmarked the address of the house, pocketed her phone, and walked to her injured friend. Luke stood over him, smiled, and kicked him in his ribs again for the fuck of it. He started his piece of shit car and drove away. When Shameka made her way to her perdiem lover, she knew Talisha was in a world of shit. Talisha had canceled her number, and deleted her Facebook page in an attempt to go underground, but Luke now had her address, and was all but guaranteed to find her now.

CHAPTER 22

LUKE TOSSED, TURNED, SWORE, and sweated in his sleep from the life-altering turmoil he was pushed into. His trials and tribulations had him knocked out, but it was at the right time. Luke needed all the rest he could get before he hit the road to Maryland. His mind was gloomy, and he vowed to get back what was stolen from him. The only upside to Talisha's grand theft was that Luke had the combination and key. If Talisha was smart, she'd use dynamite to get it open, but she wasn't. The person she bounced with might be intelligent so he knew he had to make moves.

Luke was a light sleeper. A mouse darting across the floor could wake him, but tonight, he was engaged in a nightmare, and didn't hear Ike, Toby, and the Rottweiler enter his home. They stood over Luke stone-faced. It was time for him to rise.

"Mr. Law."

Luke didn't move.

"Mr. Law," Ike said. Ike raised the volume on his voice.

Luke still remained immersed in his nightmare. Ike beckoned Toby with his eyes. On cue, Toby smacked the shit out of Luke. Luke's eyes opened, and he swiftly reached under his pillow, but grabbed a ball of air.

"Looking for this?" Ike asked as he dangled the Beretta by the gun handle. Luke's mouth remained opened, unable to understand how the two goons were able to get into his home and confiscate his rod.

"Coin?"

Luke looked into Ike's eyes and saw pure, unadulterated evil. The white fedora hat and black, tailored two-buttoned suit accentuated his muscular, slim body and hell bound spirit. Toby stood at Ike's side, dressed in similar attire minus the hat. He stood firm and tall, and held a *Targus* book bag. The dog sat in the corner. He panted and looked at Luke. Luke knew they were there to kill him. In a twisted way, Luke embraced death. The events that led Ike and Toby to his apartment were toxic enough to make a man jump off a bridge. Luke's mind was soaked with unrest.

"I guess you're going to have to kill me. I don't have it at the moment despite all the shit I've gone through to get your one point five mill." Ike sensed the sarcasm. He cracked a smile and whistled for his dog. The dog walked to Ike and sat next to his leg. The dog panted and growled, and he awaited his master's command to kill. Ike knelt down next to his best friend and petted him. The dog licked Ike's face.

"Mr. Law, Bishop here is my best friend, and I'll do anything to protect him. He would do the same for me. We love each other." Luke watched Ike's interaction with the dog, and knew Ike was out of his fucking skull, but he kept cool while Luke scanned his room. He looked for possible escape routes and weapons. If Luke were to die tonight, then one out of the three would die as well. Since he believed his early death was inevitable, Luke knew there was no point on going out like a bitch. Ike continued to play with his dog while Luke contemplated an approach.

"Ike, I'm going to keep it real with you. This dude," Luke said, nodding at Toby, "been a witness to nine lics. This motherfucker watches me from dusk 'til dawn. Me and my homeboy made cash money. If this fat piece of shit wasn't busy watching me, he would of caught the stupid bitch walking out of here with my safe."

Toby moved forward and lunged, but Ike ceased Toby's action with an open palm.

"Ike man, I know you ain't..."

"Ain't? Ain't? What is ain't? Thank goodness for your size. That will be all."

Toby humbled himself and fell back. He was insulted, but he knew better than to allow his look of contempt to be viewed by his superior; instead, Toby directed his hellish gaze on Luke. On the surface, Luke resembled a warrior taking his own death on the chin, but then an image of Baron flashed into his mind. Luke's love for life returned, though he expected death with each passing second.

Ike stood and Bishop remained by his side.

"My deepest condolences to your crime buddies. I guess being the third man to a botched robbery has its perks. You're alive. I must admit, I was very impressed by the creativity, but the gun happy lard ass used a few bullets to stop *you* from getting my money, which is why I believe its only fair that I give you a month to come up with my currency." The armor truck robbery was all over the news, but Ike's knowledge about the intricate details of the attempted heist was beyond him. Normally, he would spot Toby sitting in the car looking like a mortician in the driver seat of a hearse, but Toby wasn't at the robbery. Luke had checked thoroughly, and had seen no sign of the fuck. Luke wasn't gonna ask any questions on how Ike knew what he knew; he was being offered another chance at a dark life. The game had changed when Dan and Rosa got cut down. Luke was on his own. This time, he would include no one in his misfortune.

Satan's demons prepared themselves to leave. The dog remained seated. The dog bared his teeth and growled. Ike whistled for Bishop. The dog stopped growling, and he walked to his master. Ike turned around, and placed Luke's gun on the dresser.

"I'm sure you'll be needing this. By the way," Ike said as he walked to Luke's bedside with Bishop in tow. He kneeled down, and moved his face close to Luke's ear. "Bishop is angry Mr. Law. He's angry with your late friend Dan for killing the dog that was trying to protect his family. If *you* would have slain that dog in Meriden, I would have forgotten about Steve's debt of *one point five mill'* and donated your body to science. And for future reference, another tedious comment like the *one point five mill'* you made is a guaranteed ride to your plot. Understood?"

Luke nodded.

"August 21st, 1831, Nat Turner and his cronies went from plantation to plantation killing whites. If need be, this year, I will go from ghetto to ghetto breaking Laws. Toby, do the honors." Ike and his dog walked out of the room. Luke's heart rate reached its zenith. He knew he was done. Toby looked at him coldly. He wanted to kill Luke so bad that he caught an erection, but Toby had to follow orders and lay off the fantasy. Instead of death, Toby tossed Luke the *Targus* book bag, walked out of the room, and joined his boss and the dog in the truck. After Luke sighed and caught his breath, Luke unzipped the bag, looked in it, and vomited on himself. The grotesque and decomposed head of an opened mouth, bearded man sat smugly in the book bag.

CHAPTER 23

MOMENTS AFTER THE UNINVITED guests departed, Luke was already dressed. He glanced occasionally at the zipped *Targus* book bag and vomit on the floor. If he didn't move fast, Luke's head could be placed in another bag, and used as a deterrent for another person that faced a similar ordeal. Luke moved swiftly as he gathered his shit. When Dan flashed across his mind, Luke discarded the thought. He had plenty of time to think about that on the highway.

Minutes later, Luke was ready. His duffle bag housed his toothpaste, a washcloth, two bottles of water, one change of gear, his gun, and two boxes of bullets. Riding filthy on I-95 south was risky as fuck, but Luke's head and his loved ones eliminated his fear of capture.

Luke had enough money for food, gas, the rental, tolls, and cheap lodging. The twisted shit Ike pulled almost made Luke forget he had an unemployment check in the mailbox. Not wanting to waste anymore time, Luke walked out the door, locked it, and proceeded on his mission of getting his money back. On his way to the car, Luke stopped at the mailbox and retrieved his check. He had plenty of opportunity to get direct deposit, but never followed through. If Luke had it, he could get the rental and shoot straight to the highway. Now he had to stop at the bank to cash the check. His phone vibrated as soon as he got situated in the car. It vibrated repeatedly before Luke acknowledged it. When he did, he didn't recognize the number. He figured it was the detective that harassed him about the death in the group home. Luke wasn't in the mood for that shit, but he answered the call anyway.

"Hello?" Irritability flooded Luke's tone.

It was a collect call from Quincy Dixon, an inmate incarcerated in Enfield. It was Steve's best friend and crime partner. Luke was in a rush and wanted to get the fuck out of dodge, but Quincy called for a reason. Luke accepted the call.

"Q, what up?"

"You man. No time for formalities. I sent two letters to Dan's crib. I see you never got them." Quincy had urgency in his voice.

"Dan mentioned it, but we never got around it. I didn't know you sent a second letter. What's good though?"

"Luke, go get the letters. Read the second letter last. Its labeled number two. I just sent that. Will hit you in forty-five minutes. If you out of town, get back in it. I'm out." The phone disconnected.

"Quincy! Fuck!" Luke tossed the phone to the passenger seat. He didn't know what Quincy was up to, but Quincy picked a fucked up time to be on some mystery shit. Luke had to get his cash. Lives were on the line.

It took Luke eight attempts to get his car started. His cell phone vibrated again. Luke fumbled the phone before he got it steady. He thought it was Quincy calling back, but it was Zora. Luke was gonna answer it. He missed her. Her voice was a remedy that eased his sanity, and shone a bright light on the darkest corner of his heart, but Luke had to let the call go to voicemail.

After dealing with Rhonda's displaced anger, she gave Luke the letters. Luke cashed his check, and he picked up the rental. He gassed up the gray Ford Focus, drove it to Lakewood Park, and parked it next to the basketball court. The cell phone buzzed again. Luke didn't bother to see who it was; instead, he picked up one of the letters and opened it.

I hope you are mentally prepared to hear this shit. If not, fuck it. You need to know what I know and keep this shit hush. After you read this letter, burn it.

Luke stopped reading for a second, took a deep breath, prepared himself for bad news, and looked around for Toby. The coast was clear. He picked up the letter and continued.

NEXT OF KIN

Instead of small talk, I'm going to cut straight to the chase. Omar killed Steve bro.

Luke read the line again to see if what he read was official. He dropped the letter in his lap, and trembled. Tears of rage spilled from Luke's eyes. His teeth gnawed on his bottom lip. He continued to ignore his phone, and Luke continued.

Omar got bagged for carrying a loaded pistol a week after coming out of jail. Since he just finished a four-year bid, he made bail and fought his case from the outside. At his third court date, he was offered six years for the pistol, but wasn't satisfied with the offer. Omar's public defender managed to obtain another court date despite the judge's reluctance. Feeling the pressure by the six years hanging over his head, Omar snitched on Steve, and put Steve's drug operation on blast. That's why he only did three years.

The strain on Luke's face increased as he read on. According to the rest of the letter, Omar used Timmy Blairwood for the set up. Steve didn't know of Omar's betrayal, but Omar knew Steve would kill him if he ever caught wind. Steve had no idea that police were hip to him. Omar knew he cowardly fucked Steve over, and knew it would be a matter of time before Steve went down. Guilt ridden and paranoid, Omar was fearful of being labeled a snitch, and he made a vital decision to kill Steve rather than him spend the rest of his life in prison based off of Omar's testimony.

Omar wanted to set up a nest egg when he returned to society since he had a month before he started his three year bid. Omar knew Steve was headed to New Jersey to score something big in the next three days. That was his chance. Omar planned to kill two birds with one stone. After Omar robbed and killed Steve, he attended the funeral, disappeared with the work, flipped it twice, stashed his money before going away for three years for the gun, and started a new life in Maryland. Since Omar was flashy, he posted cars, jewelry, and all types of signs of lavish living on Facebook and Instagram after he finished the three-year bid. Timmy was guilt ridden, and he told someone he thought he trusted. Quincy found out a month and a half ago, and he tossed out a previous theory about Steve's death, but Quincy didn't mention that in the kite. Luke could had found out sooner if Dan remembered to give him the letter.

Luke's anger reached its boiling point after he finished the letter. He always saw Timmy in passing, and wrote him off as a druggie, but

Luke knew Timmy's guilt forced him into a world of addiction. Either way, in Luke's mind, Timmy lived on borrowed time. Luke was so occupied by the revelation that he didn't connect Maryland, Omar, and Talisha together. He wondered if Talisha was with him, but stopped that thought when he looked at the second letter labeled number two.

Luke read the second letter quickly. Quincy perceived Luke as a Catholic schooled, college bound square. Quincy knew Luke as Steve's baby brother. That didn't stop Quincy from providing his proposal. Luke held the second letter and nodded because it involved big money. When Quincy provided the address, Luke's hunch that Talisha was with him was confirmed; the address in Shameka's IPhone matched.

Luke needed to be in Maryland within the next five or six hours, but he had to stick around for a while. He drove away from the park distraught and fatigued. When the memory of Dan's cut down corpse swept into his mind, Luke blocked the visual and lit a roach clip. He peered at the rearview mirror still looking for Toby, but there was no sign of him. Luke cut a left, made an immediate right, and kept straight until he reached his destination. He waited outside the house until Quincy called as promised.

"Yes, I accept."

"If you there, you'll get that in the next five minutes. If not, it's all good. It will get done regardless," Quincy said. Quincy gave Luke more coded instruction before the call ended.

Five minutes later, the two cronies Quincy described walked to the car, told Luke to pop the trunk, dropped a duffel bag into it, closed it, and went on their way. Quincy's timing and his ability to operate from the inside were impressive. Luke hoped he wasn't on phone review, even though the conversation was short, discreet, and coded. Luke left the front of the three-family house and made moves. While in motion, Luke knew it was time to talk to Wil. He had to swallow his pride. He needed Wil to protect Baron and his mother. Wil was a retired cop. Luke was taking a risk if he talked to former law enforcement, but he had no choice. With that thought in mind, Zora sent an alarming text.

CHAPTER 24

WIL AND LUKE CLEARED the air, and then Luke got straight to the point, telling Wil exactly what was going on, and gave Wil sole responsibility for the protection of his loved ones. Renee told Wil she had a strong hunch that Luke was into something shady, but Wil never imagined death being involved. Luke told Wil the story like a raconteur. It was six-thirty in the evening, and Renee was due home anytime. Dressed in windbreaker pants and a gray t-shirt, Wil stood up and beckoned Luke to the sliding backdoor. Once outside, the men stood squarely facing one another. Wil pulled a pack of Newport out of his pocket. Luke didn't smoke cigarettes, but he gladly accepted one from Wil when he offered.

"One point five million or die, huh?" Will asked.

"Yeah."

"So Luke, let me get this straight. Are you telling me that we are all in danger because of your brother's debt?"

"That's exactly what I'm telling you."

The autumn wind blew leaves all over the deck. Wil still tried to make sense of what Luke told him. Wil took a drag off his cigarette, and exhaled smoke into the cool evening. Silence drifted between the men. Luke glanced at his watch, and he cringed at the time that was being wasted.

"Look, we have to be smart. We need to call the police and..."

"Wil, you ain't hearing me. If you call the police, we'll all be dead in a matter of days."

"But Luke..."

"I'm starting to lose the little patience I have." Luke was getting agitated. Wil was his only option to protect his family, and he was already trying to include his cop buddies.

"Alright man, just relax. I'll call Morales at the station and have him check the New Jersey database for Ike Collins. I'm sure they can get him on something. He'll be off the street in no time," Wil said like it wasn't a big deal.

Luke flicked his cigarette butt onto the deck, grabbed Wil by his t-shirt, shoved him against the sliding door, pulled out his gun, and placed it in the middle of his chest. Wil could hold his own and knew martial arts, but the crazed look Luke wore on his face confirmed the seriousness of the problem.

"Dan and Rosa got killed in that attempted robbery! Guess what? *I* was the third man in that shit! Me and Dan robbed the group homes. If my mom told you *anything* about me, she told you I could do anything I want, and that my brain is my greatest asset. If you believe her, do you think I will help rob a cash truck without a motive behind it?"

"Luke, I got it. I won't say a thing, but take the gun off me."

Luke and Wil heard Renee walk through the front door. Luke put his gun away and dashed to the small trailhead in the backyard that led to another street. By the time Renee made it to the deck, Luke was out of sight. While Renee shared the details of her day, Luke's words echoed in Wil's head. Wil had to tell her.

"Now do you think I was trying to play you Zora?"

"Luke, I know, but how do you expect me to relax when there's a scary looking man camped out across the street?" Zora was teary eyed and petrified. She thought Luke had exaggerated his story to have an excuse not to be with her, but Ike and Toby confirmed it to her. Zora been holed up in her apartment all day, and she peeked occasionally through the blinds to check for movement. She checked two hours ago, and the black truck was gone. When Zora checked again, the black truck was back, but Toby was alone.

"Because he's not going to do anything. Him being outside your crib is my reminder to come up with that dough." Zora sat down and wept. Luke sat beside her and held her. He took in her apartment, and didn't find much entertainment besides a twenty-seven inch Vizio. Since Zora didn't have cable, she relied on her jail broken *Amazon Fire TV Stick* to help her kill time. It was the first time Luke stepped into her residence, and hopefully not the last. Whether Zora wanted to be with Luke or not, she was involved because of association. Luke did the only thing he knew to be right. He pulled his gun from the holster and extended it to her. Zora looked at it like it was toxic, but he forced it into her hand.

"Take it Zora. You see how you're indirectly involved? That's how I feel. It's not fair, but we were forced into the game."

Zora pried away. Her eyes burned fanatically.

"No Luke, you met me knowing you were going through this shit! Now that asshole and his friend know where I live! And for that, you owe me. You need to stay here and protect me. That's the *least* you can do!" Her eyeliner was smeared because of her tears.

"Zora, I gave you a loaded gun. I would love to stay here and protect you, but that bitch went down south with my safe and I have to get it back."

"So you're going down south not sure if your safe still exists?"

"It's a chance I have to take."

"How much exactly is in that safe Luke?"

"The less you know, the better."

The botched robbery on the news seeped into Zora's mind.

"Were you there when your friend got killed?"

She was fishing.

"I got to go Zora. The sooner I leave, the sooner I'll be back."

Zora pivoted her body. "Can I come with you?"

"No. I'm not sure if I'll even come back here alive, and I'll be damned if you lose your life in the process. Look baby, I have to do this. There are no options. It's live or die. Right now, the only thing I'm asking for is for you to trust me. I know this shit is crazy, but that's the reality of it."

Luke and Zora hugged. Zora didn't want to let him go.

"I love you," Zora said. She planted a wet kiss on his lips.

Luke was taken aback.

"I...I love you too Zora."

Filled with fear, she wept in his arms.

"I'm going to text you Wil's number. I will text him while I'm on the road so he will know who is texting him. You and him are the only ones that know, even though after tonight, my mom is going to blow my phone up because Wil has to tell her. Remember, alerting police will draw the end of our lives. As far as the gun I'm leaving, don't touch it unless you plan on using it."

"I got you baby. Please be careful and come back in one piece," Zora said before she let Luke go.

When Luke walked out the door, Zora wondered if it would be the last time she would ever see him.

CHAPTER 25

Six days later

A HALF CRESCENT MOON covered the early morning. It was a little after midnight. Clinton, Maryland was quiet and void. The crickets communicated with one another. The residential neighborhood was high end. Manicured lawns and shrubbery surrounded the modernly built homes. The neighborhood was swank. Talisha couldn't believe she was in it. She'd never been out of Connecticut, and only saw lavish surroundings on television or magazines. Despite her high level of comfort, regret flooded Talisha's mind as she sniffed and sucked cocaine off of Omar's dick. Omar grabbed the little hair she had and fucked her mouth. Omar's penis grew larger at the sight of the unopened safe sitting in the corner of the bedroom. Omar pumped her grill three more times before he fired a load down her throat. Omar Thompson rose from the bed, and he went to the bathroom. Talisha remained on the bed, flustered with guilt. She'd left her life and child for a fling. Since Omar was unattractive, his money compensated for it.

While she entertained regretful thoughts, Omar walked out of the bathroom fully clothed. His Tru Religion dark blue jeans, gray hoodie, and the thick golden link around his neck spelled money, but the scars, blemishes, razor bumps, and acne on his face killed the outfit. Omar rubbed cocoa butter on his gaunt face and baldhead. His imperfections glistened because of his light skin. Talisha looked at him and cringed. She made a huge mistake. Her face involuntarily shifted into a snarl.

"What's wrong with you?"

"Nothing," Talisha lied. "Why do you keep asking me that?"

"I don't be asking you. You had a suspect look on your face so I questioned it."

Talisha resumed her front, and she crawled seductively across the bed towards him. Omar's manhood stiffened. The sight of her naked body turned him on. Talisha wasn't blessed with the body of a model, but she knew she could seduce him. Omar's feelings got involved before he started fucking her. She knew she had Omar wide open. Omar was ugly as shit, but his greenbacks were a thing of beauty. The safe was the exclamation point.

"Baby, are we going to try to crack this safe?" Talisha asked as she unbuckled his pants.

"Yes baby, that's the plan," Omar said. He turned Talisha around, entered her, and fucked her for a few minutes before he ejaculated into her. The sharp, solid knock on the door didn't stop Omar from getting his nut. The knocking persisted as he took his time cleaning off the smell of sex from his body. He left Talisha in the bedroom, and he opened the door.

"What the fuck y'all niggas knocking so hard for? What the fuck? A nigga can't even get his shit off without motherfuckers pounding on the door."

"My bad Omar. We thought something was up," Jose said. Jose was a burly, sleek Hispanic man in this mid twenties. Jose towered over his superior. Omar was of average height and frail, but Jose was afraid of him. Omar was grimy, and he did whatever he had to do to outmaneuver his enemies. Leonard, a corn rowed dark skin man, was Omar's height, but a tad stockier. He didn't fear Omar like his partner Jose did, but he fed his boss with a long spoon. Omar was a crooked, paranoid, morally debased individual who'd use anyone as a human chess piece.

"Why the fuck would something be up?" Omar looked at Jose coldly.

"Nah yo, nothin' like that. This game we playin' is serious bro." Jose ran out of words. Leonard hated every minute of the exchange, but Jose wasn't putting money in his pocket. Leonard told Jose to cut the extra commentary out and stick to business, but Jose was afraid of Omar, and Jose had a hard time composing himself around him.

NEXT OF KIN

"What game we playing?"

"Look man, we just came here to pick up the shit and be out," Leonard voiced. He took the pressure off of Jose.

Omar mean mugged the low level soldiers like they were beneath scum. He kept his glare on Jose, but decided to keep his bullying to a minimum. After all, Omar had a woman who he thought the world of in his bedroom.

"Nutty and Stacks is going to D.C. for the pick-up. Look for a Black Cadillac Deville. Hop in, make the transaction, and they'll drop you scumbags off to another car. It's a beat up brown Honda. Get in it, hit Silver Springs, and bring a *ki* to Eloy. Done deal."

Omar handed the men the drugs, and told them to kick rocks. After closing the front door on their backs, he shifted his attention back to the safe and Talisha.

Nutty and Stacks shared a bottle of Wild Turkey over a game of chess. They had hours to kill before their run. The men took swigs from the bottle, and they competed with one another. Nutty was a tall, caramel colored twenty-eight year old that sported a mini-afro. Stacks was around the same age. He was short, light skinned, and stocky. Stacks wiped beads of sweat from his brow because they played for money. Bundles of dope, blood money, and a few guns decorated the counters and floors in the garage of the safe house. The men were reckless and lawless. The amount of product and guns on the property was equal to a life sentence for a persistent felon. The men remained focused on their game until they heard glass shatter in the house. They instinctively drew their weapons and made moves.

Meanwhile, Luke had to hurry. He ran around the safe house, and then slid underneath the garage door. He ignored the cash and money and stuck to the plan. Luke thought the plan would take a long time to execute, but his chance came in the form of a bottle of liquor. He knew his window of opportunity was closing rapidly, and it was only a matter of time before the men returned. Luke fished in his pocket, withdrew a quarter ounce size bag of arsenic, poured it in the liquor bottle, shook it, and dashed out of the garage. The men returned a few minutes later having found nothing in the house, but were still riddled with

113

suspicion. Nutty and Stacks sat, drank, and resumed their game of chess.

...

Luke waited patiently for the man known as Stacks to stop moving and breathing. The emotions of taking two lives didn't sink in. Luke had no feelings. He needed his safe, and the treasure in the garage. The poisoned men were in his way. Quincy wanted Luke to plant a gun used in a murder in Omar's house and mission complete. Quincy didn't know about Talisha, her rendezvous with Omar, or Luke's ordeal with Ike, but the men had something in common that concerned Omar's household; they had business there and most importantly, Omar killed Steve. Since Quincy mentioned muscle in the letter, Luke contacted one of Dan's old connects while en route to Maryland, and made a stop in Queens. Luke copped the powerful dose of arsenic on consignment on the strength of Dan. Eliminating Omar's muscle quietly instead of drawing blood from gunplay was more logical.

Feces, vomit, and blood pooled around the bodies. The amount of arsenic Luke poured in the bottle was enough to kill an elephant. The stench was unbearable. Luke moved around the messy bodies, and he gathered the goods. Now it was on to his unopened safe. Luke watched Omar for hours trying to open it. Luke didn't want to leave no time for Omar to become creative. In six days, Luke found Omar and Talisha, followed Omar's muscle, crept near them, peeped their dialogue, picked up on habits, and had the rest of their routine imprinted in the back of his mind. The amount of cash and drugs in the bag was uncounted, but killing the men provided Luke a cash bonus.

When Luke placed the last stack of cash in the bag, another one of Omar's goons walked casually through the door that led to the garage, and thought he was next in line for a game of chess. Instead, the goon found two of his homeboys sprawled out on the floor covered in their own bodily fluids. The crony had left his gun in his car. Luke pulled his out, but his adrenaline made him unsteady, and he dropped it. Big man charged at Luke and grabbed him. The unknown crony was incredibly strong, and Luke felt it in his grip. The man punched, kicked, and hurled Luke against the garage walls. Tools, the drug and cash filled duffle bag, and other miscellaneous shit fell to the floor as the burly man continued to rough Luke up. The man grabbed

Luke by his shirt collar, and hurled him against another wall. Luke was beaten up and weak, and tasted his own blood. Smelling defeat, big dude went in for the kill. Big man choked Luke. The look in the big man's eyes was intense as he covered Luke's throat with his beefy hands. Luke found enough strength in his left hand to secure the long folding knife he had in his back pocket. The man squeezed Luke's neck until he felt the sharpness of a blade. Luke rammed it repeatedly into the man's gut. The big man felt the pain instantly, and it caused him to loosen his hold on Luke's neck. Luke poked thirty-nine holes in the burly man until he folded. The big man grimaced from the pain, and he coughed up blood as his body involuntarily jerked. He was dying. Luke struggled to rise from his position, barely able to stand on his feet. Luke winced, grunted, and groaned. The man's beady eyes pleaded with him, but Luke avoided any form of mercy. Luke stabbed the man until he stopped moving.

Luke was still masked and gloved when he made his way out of the garage covered in blood, vomit, and feces. An hour later, Luke was in Omar's home in the clothes he had on when his feet touched Maryland soil. Luke now wore a different ski mask, leather black gloves, and possessed a heart full of hatred.

At two o'clock in the morning, as expected, Omar and Talisha slept soundly in the king-sized bed. The pair drank, drugged, and fucked their way to sleep. Talisha lay naked, her right leg crossed over Omar's naked body. Luke stood over them bruised, scarred, and furious. Steve's voice and guidance filled his mind with memories. Luke wanted to kill Omar. Although he'd come to terms with Talisha's cheating, it was still a blow to Luke's pride to see her infidelity displayed in front of him. Luke contemplated on putting a hole in both of them, but the knowledge of what Quincy had in store for Omar stopped him from doing it. Luke planted the gun in the house, and left with the safe.

CHAPTER 26

THE MOTEL IN BALTIMORE was a hole in the wall piece of shit. The mattress was flat and uncomfortable, but it didn't stop Luke from counting cash on it. After he soaked in the bathtub for an hour, the water therapy did nothing for his bruised ribs. Luke's face had massive bruising, but he was alive, and his safe was in the trunk of the rental. He counted ninety-three thousand dollars, and a hundred-twenty thousand in drugs from the safe house.

The two Percocet Luke swallowed helped with the pain. The weed he smoked numbed the intensity of his conscious; however, the mere thought of life imprisonment for three bodies scared Luke, but it was necessary. Protecting his family from harm was a bigger necessity. Luke did what he had to do, and he would do it again. Ike was serious about his cash. Luke didn't know whose head he chopped off, but he didn't want Ike to use his own head as a scare tactic for someone else.

A cloud of anger surfaced from the thought of Omar. It wasn't a surprise. Steve always told Luke the dudes who were afraid of you would never hesitate to cut your throat given the opportunity. Omar had been terrified of Steve since childhood. Omar always fronted like Steve was his best friend, but he hated and feared him. Omar hated the fact that he always borrowed light from Steve's shine. Omar carried his hatred for Steve for years. Steve was headstrong, and he said whatever crossed his mind without reservation. Omar never had the heart and balls to address Steve whenever he felt crossed.

After Luke placed the money and drugs back in the bag, it was time to head back to Connecticut. Lingering around could be fatal. He punched his address into the GPS, and he was set to go. Luke had plenty of road ahead of him to think of a lic. He'd made progress, but he wasn't there yet. Luke sat at the foot of the bed, and he scrolled through the GPS Dan left him. Luke clicked onto an address Dan spoke of a few days before being cut down. Dan said it was an easy lic if done correctly. Luke felt the pain in his body, particularly his ribs, and he wondered if he had it in him to pull it off. Luke looked at his chrome and pearl-handled thirty-eight, and he figured he had nothing to lose.

Bikers occupied the dingy tavern. They watched highlights of the Sprint Cup Series while hunched over their beer and liquor. Cigarette smoke spread through the shit hole as the shaggy, bearded, leather clad men congregated around the horseshoe bar. A large confederate flag covered the top of the front entrance. The stuffed moose head on the wall behind the bar looked like it kept watch over everyone.

Hilton poured himself and Taylor a shot of whisky amidst the cheers and jeers. Hilton, a burly man with scraggly hair, a Nazi symbol on the side of his neck, and a handlebar mustache, owned the bar. Taylor accepted the drink with a vague look on his face.

"You should supply the Oxidado to the coons. Let them niggers kill off their own," Taylor said.

"Wish it was that simple, but it ain't. The Puerto Rican gang out here got a hold of it, sold it in their community, and five of them died from it within the last two weeks. Pablo and Juan received manslaughter charges for selling that shit. The ones that avoided jail time all dropped dead. Its extremely profitable, but the niggers and spics won't touch it."

Hilton and Taylor threw back another shot. The men small talked some more before Dolly, a petite, freckled red head waitress, rushed behind the bar.

"Hilton, you better check this out!"

Hilton and Taylor, along with three other bikers, rushed behind Dolly to the back room. The men gathered around the camera in the backroom, and they saw a masked man prowling around the dumpster in the alley.

"Go get Teddy and Hank. We have ourselves an intruder to fry," Hilton said icily.

Harley Davidsons were lined up in a row outside the bar. Luke crept around the joint. He moved around the club with patience, but the only way he was gonna pull off the lik was if he snatched a hostage. Luke didn't see a biker outside. The voice in his head told him he needed to get out of there, but the other voice reminded him of the eminent danger his family was in. Either way, Luke came for the Oxidado, even though that shit would bring death to every fiend in Waterbury. The demand for the powerful narcotic was high, but Luke's morale was running on fumes.

Luke saw an opening. He spotted a dumpster. That was his key to the window five feet over it. The set up looked obvious, but he didn't see any other way. He jumped onto the dumpster, but the bullet that whizzed a millimeter away from his temple made him fall head first to the ground. Luke was hurt, but he gathered enough strength to roll out of the gunman's view. Blood oozed out of the open wound on the right side of his forehead. Luke had a large cut from his spill to the ground, and a huge knot over his left eye. Luke took out his gun from his black hoodie, cocked it, and fired blindly. The shaggy hair biker held his Glock nine out the window, and fired another shot. Luke grimaced at the sound of the blast. He heard the other bikers rev up their Harleys. If Luke remained crouched behind the dumpster, he would join Steve in Heaven or Hell. The car was a half block away. Wasting no more time, Luke fired another shot in the direction of the window, ran fast from his position, and weaved back and forth to make it more difficult for the gunman to draw another bead.

However, bikers were in motion, and they were closing in on his ass. The bikers fired off a volley of shots. It was a cacophony of Harley Davidson engines and bullets. Luke turned the corner of the alley and gained more ground, but the distance between Luke and the bikers shortened. Bullets continued to fly. The bullets pierced cars, buildings, and an innocent bystander. There was a decent amount of people in the vicinity, but Luke was perceived as a blur, and he ran for his life. Luke's adrenaline was so high that he didn't feel the pain in his bruised ribs, but the pain in his head and face was excruciating. Sparks from the bullets that pierced the streets gave Luke multiple reality checks. The bikers would not let up. Luke weaved to the far left, ran a few thousand feet, and made an abrupt turn in the direction of the rental. He threw the bikers off for a second, but time was still scarce. Luke ran as fast as he could. He braced for the burn of a bullet, but luckily, he wasn't hit.

Once inside the car, Luke turned the ignition, ducked, and drove blindly into traffic. He clipped a few cars as bullets shattered the windows and windshield. When Luke finally got the car straight, it was a high-speed chase. Pedestrians ran behind cars, and sought every safe haven possible. Luke heard the faint sounds of sirens off in the distance, but it wasn't a relief. He had money, drugs, and weapons in the bullet-ridden car. Fortunately, the bikers heard the sirens as well, and they aborted their mission to kill. Luke drove a half mile away from the sirens, pulled over, caught his breath, opened his safe, stashed the money and dope underneath his clothes, gathered the other bag of drugs and money, closed the empty safe, flipped the two bags over his shoulder, took off his ski mask, replaced it with a North Face skully, planted his loaded gun in the big pocket of his black hoodie, ditched the empty safe, got back into the car, drove another two miles, pulled over again, took the keys out of the ignition, and proceeded through the dark, cold streets of Baltimore on foot. It was three in the morning, and it was thirty degrees. Not knowing which way was up, Luke knew he had to devise an exit strategy fast.

CHAPTER 27

An hour later

THE COLD WIND PRESSED against Luke's battered face while he footed the hard, dangerous streets of Baltimore. The pain in his ribs worsened with each step. Dried blood stained his face, and his painful walk was noticeable from a distance. Luke walked slowly past drug dealers and goons; however, three young thugs attempted to try him because of his unsteady gait, but one of them had a trained eye. Luke never took his right hand out of the big pocket of his oversized, black hoodie, and one of the young thugs noticed it. He beckoned his boys elsewhere, and kept it moving.

Luke checked into the Motel 6 on Bloomfield Avenue after he got First aid supplies from the corner bodega. After getting the key to the room, a rail thin, dark-skinned prostitute with a blond wig emerged from the darkness of the parking lot, hoping she could score some warmth for a few hours. Luke made sure he didn't establish eye contact with her. Once inside the room, Luke dropped the bags. He looked out the window for the hooker, potential followers, and bikers. He had cold, hard cash, bricks of coke, and a loaded weapon on him, and Luke didn't need anymore unnecessary shit. Luke didn't want to drop more bodies, but he would if he had to.

Lukc bandaged himself the best he could. It wasn't a great job, but the work he did to clean himself was enough to stop the bleeding. The pain in his ribs subsided because of the Percocet, but Luke was still stuck in Baltimore. He cursed himself for being greedy, and Luke acknowledged that he was lucky; death had missed him by an inch. Luke was choked, and was fired at by men who carried an array of guns. He was banged up, and could barely move. The high speed running he'd done put pressure on his ribs.

Luke lay on the bed, puffed on a Black and Mild, and reached for the prepaid he'd bought from the bodega before he winced in pain. He moved slowly off of the bed, and he opened one of the bags. Luke pulled out the other prepaid phone, and sat slowly back down on the bed. He didn't want to involve her, but Zora was his only hope of getting out of Maryland quietly, safely, and quickly.

The dental office was busy. Senior citizens watched television, new patients filled out paperwork, a young businessman spoke loudly on his cell phone, and patients read magazines while they waited. Zora was on the phone scheduling and confirming appointments. She moved at a feverish pace, but it helped keep her mind off of Luke. Zora had to admit; she should have never gone deep with him, but she had, and now, she was gravely concerned about him. Zora hadn't heard from him in a week, and she feared the worst. She developed a friendship with Wil, and she shared her concerns with him. Zora hadn't slept or eaten adequately since Luke left for Maryland. She spent the last few nights holding a gun, even though the man parked outside her home had left when Luke departed.

"Thursday? Let's see, we have a 9:30 and a 2:00. Friday is full. Two o'clock?"

After she confirmed an appointment with the patient, Zora felt her phone vibrate in her pocket. She knew it was Luke because he gave her the prepaid phone for only him to call on it. The office phone rang at the same time. Zora beckoned her co-worker to take the call. She grabbed her jacket, rushed through the waiting area, and stepped into the frigid weather.

"Baby?"

"Zora, I need your help. Listen carefully..."

Dan's voice made Luke sweat, toss, and turn in the midst of his nightmare, but it was the sound of the gunshot that jarred him out of his sleep. Perspiration dripped down Luke's neck, and onto his chest. Luke panted like he'd just run a marathon. His nightmare of Dan getting clipped reoccurred daily, but it was something Luke had to live with. The loud thud Rosa's body made when she was cut down sometimes disturbed Luke's peace, but he had to wage war against the past. If he didn't, Luke was a dead man.

When Luke heard the loud, sharp knock, he instinctively gripped the weapon that was underneath his pillow, struggled out of the bed, and inched himself to the door with the gun pointed at it. Luke was edgy, scared, paranoid, and on point. The pain in his ribs screamed when he walked to the door. When Luke looked through the peephole, he realized he'd slept for hours. With the gun still in his hand, he unlocked and opened the door. Zora stood at her full height as she eyed every bruise, cut, and wound on his face and body. She was a Godsend in Luke's eyes. Luke looked behind her, scanned the parking lot, and guided her in. The formalities and embrace were short-lived because of the pain in his ribs, but Zora cried and kissed him despite his head and body being in a war. Zora never understood her strange attraction to Luke, but she knew he looked at her like no other man. The danger that lurked around Luke was frightening and exciting, but either way, she had Luke's back until the end. She was in love with him.

Luke and Zora locked eyes. Zora held both of her hands on her face and lost it. She buried her head in his chest as Luke stroked her hair. Luke cracked his chipped tooth smile. She was a ride or die chick, and Luke cherished the air she breathed, and the ground she walked on. If Luke and his family made it out alive, Zora would be his wife one day. Luke would die before he allowed Ike and Toby to slaughter those he cherished.

"Zora, I really appreciate you coming through for me, but right now, we gotta dip."

She gathered herself.

"Baby, what happened?"

Luke looked at her long and hard, but he knew he would have to take what happened tonight to the grave with him.

"The most important thing here is that I'm alive, and I got my stash back, but on the real, some things are better left unsaid."

NEXT OF KIN

Zora stopped questioning him out of respect. She understood the game, and she knew Luke was only protecting her. Without another word, Zora handed Luke the car keys, and she collected his belongings because of his condition. After gathering the goods, Luke checked out of the motel, and they hit the road to Connecticut.

CHAPTER 28

Waterbury, Connecticut

AT 10:30PM, local police received a tip from a drifter about a body. Police, German Shepherds, and other officials made their way through the small trailhead with flashlights on North Walnut Street en route to the body at 11:00pm. The weather was brisk and windy. They didn't know if the caller was credible, but they had to acknowledge it. A thirty-one year old male had fallen off the grid a little under a month ago.

Grumbles, politics, radio, and gruff police talk echoed through the air as they walked far through the wooded area headed towards City Mills. The long walk was uneventful until the German Shepherds pulled on their chains, steering their masters to the left. They walked through thick shrubbery. The voices ceased because the dogs smelled something. The dogs walked the police through more rough terrain where they discovered a decomposed, skeletal faced, greenish colored corpse. It was lying prone, undisturbed, and facedown tangled in the bushes.

Detectives collected fragile evidence from the body, and they noted that it was doused with insect repellant to mask the smell of decomposition. The cadaver was photographed, logged, and tagged before it was placed inside the coroner's van.

Talisha and Omar sat rigidly upright on the large sectional, smoking a stick of piff, and wondering who could have stolen the safe a few days ago. Omar hadn't seen Nutty, Stacks, and Mike in two days, and Omar had a hunch they stole it. Even though it belonged to Luke, Omar didn't once think Luke was responsible for the grand theft. Omar always knew Luke to be a lame, so it never crossed his mind. He thought clearly about the usual passerby's who frequented his home. Talisha, on the other hand, knew it was Luke thanks to the Facebook inbox message she'd received from Shameka. Talisha figured heavy money had to be in the safe for Luke to pursue Shameka for the address, and to pistol-whip her friend Kirby into a concussion. Talisha decided to keep that to herself. It wiped some of the guilt she had for leaving Luke, and most importantly, her son.

Talisha pulled the piff moderately. She kept her head numb to mask her regret leaving Baron, but the love Talisha had for Luke was long gone. Luke and Talisha's personalities didn't match, and they constantly clashed. In Luke's and everyone's perspective, Talisha was useless. She didn't possess the tools, wits, and credentials to stand a chance in a custody battle. Talisha was a high school dropout, jobless, and her urine was filthy from years of weed. Now that Talisha fulfilled her wish of running away, the terrible mistake she'd made kept her up at night.

The LED light on Omar's phone flashed. Without screening the call, he spoke into it.

"Who the fuck is this?"

Omar listened intensely as Leonard shared the news about Stacks, Nutty, and Mike's deaths. Leonard and Jose laid low since they discovered the bodies. Leonard told him that he thought the men were poisoned because of the vomit, body fluids, and feces next to their corpses, but Mike, the big, solid Haitian, was stabbed to death. Omar's mind scrambled for answers, but came up with no solution. That explained their disappearance. Now it was the issue of the safe. Omar placed Leonard and Jose on notice, but didn't warn or tell them since he just heard a powerful dose of bad news. Omar had no idea what he was dealing with. He began to feel cagey and paranoid. Omar brought those men everywhere he went. Now he felt the cold chill of being exposed and vulnerable. Whoever murdered Omar's crew could be aiming for him next. He didn't plan on sticking around. Omar planned to be out of the house in a matter of minutes. As soon as he ended the call, Omar snatched Talisha from her position and flung her against the wall.

"Who the fuck followed us down here?" He was so shaken that saliva formed in the corner of his mouth. Talisha was horrified. The look in Omar's eyes spelled murder. She'd never seen that look, and Talisha was fearful for her life.

Talisha's eyes bulged with fright. "What are you talking about? Please let me go! Please!"

Omar looked at the terror in her eyes, brought himself down, and let her go. He was out of drugs, money, and muscle. Talisha remained against the wall and she fixed her attire, and put herself back in order. Omar was panic stricken, and he was drenched with sweat.

"Omar, what happened?" She disregarded his assault, and became curious.

Omar rubbed his eyes with the base of his palms. His hands stopped the rubbing motion, and he pushed them deep in his sockets. "Stacks, Nutty, and Mike dead, that's what happened."

Talisha was afraid and confused. She thought about Luke, and the time he spent with Dan before his death. She remembered his swollen face. Luke would leave at two or three o' clock in the morning, and be gone all day. Talisha knew he was seeing another woman, but she had a feeling he was into something foul, dirty, and big. Talisha recalled his dark behavior after Dan was murdered, and she theorized that Luke was the third man on the attempted money truck robbery. She still thought the money from the attempted robbery was in the safe despite news reporters emphasizing no money lost. Either Luke made off with some of the dough, or he'd been on a mission to get it. Talisha didn't, however, think he was behind the murders. She thought that the incidents were separate and unrelated.

Talisha had a quizzical look on her face. "What?"

"You heard me. And we're next if we don't bail. Get your shit, and let's go!"

Talisha didn't know the men Omar staffed, but she had a sense that it was close to home. Omar looked like he'd spotted a shark in open water. He looked terrified, and ready to get the fuck out of dodge. Without asking any stupid questions, Talisha ran for the bedroom and started to gather drugs and her shit. Omar screamed for her to grab the kilos, and the two nine millimeters. Images of Baron flashed through her mind as she lived out the dumbest decision she'd ever made.

When they opened the front door to skip town, Clinton, Maryland police flanked Omar's manicured lawn. More cruisers arrived as their backup. Omar looked stunned as an officer showed him the warrant to search his premises, which included the bags the pair carried with them. Unfortunately, Talisha's bag contained the cocaine and guns. Lone tears slid down her face as the chapter of her life as a free woman came to an abrupt end.

"This shit is his! Omar, tell them!" Talisha barked as the slim black officer closest to her read her the Miranda rights, and placed her in handcuffs.

Omar cowardly turned his head away from her, and continued to argue with the Hispanic officer. Talisha's words turned into muffles when the officer closed the door to the cruiser.

"What the fuck is this all about?" Omar asked belligerently.

"Timothy Blairwood. That's what this is all about. Police found his body two days ago in Waterbury, Connecticut. Thanks to the judge, we have the pleasure of tearing up your home," the Hispanic officer said sarcastically.

Omar said nothing after the crude statement. After he eliminated Timmy from the planet for running his mouth about Steve's murder, he realized that the word of him killing Steve was still alive. Omar knew Quincy pulled some strings from afar, and more than likely had a tail on him. Omar felt confident that the pigs had nothing on him, but his confidence went out the window thirty minutes later when a buzzed cut officer walked out of the house with a smirk on his face. In his latex gloved hand, the police officer held a plastic bag that held the weapon Omar used to murder Tim. Bagging Talisha and dragging her out of state sealed Omar's fate.

After being read his rights, handcuffed, and led into the cruiser, Omar considered all the circumstances, and it began with Talisha. At that moment, the pieces to the puzzle fit perfectly. Omar felt in his bones that Luke planted the gun, and was behind the safe being missing. He still didn't think Luke had it in him to murder, or did he? He hadn't spoken to Luke in years, but Omar understood that the hearts of men change over time. And then he wondered if Luke knew he killed his brother. Bedding Talisha didn't help matters either. With all things considered, Luke was considered suspect. Luke had a clear and uncut motive to destroy him, and Omar knew it.

CHAPTER 29

LUKE AND ZORA WERE naked and cuddled under the thick comforter after a passionate session of lovemaking at the *Water's Edge Resort and Spa* in Westbrook, Connecticut. Zora's leg was wrapped over his, her arm lay across Luke's chest, and her angelic face remained a hair away from the side of his neck. Chemistry was tight between them. Zora's beauty and personality enticed Luke to emerge from his dark world of murder, but he remained trapped there. Toby had vanished without a trace, but Luke still wouldn't let his guard down. Luke and Wil kept constant tabs on one another. Wil took Renee out of town for a few days, but they were due back tomorrow. Wil was doing a good job protecting Baron and Renee, but Wil was running out of excuses. Wil told Luke he wanted to come clean, but Luke persisted *he* would tell her when they get back in from town.

The bumping, grinding, and position shifting took a small toll on Luke's bruised ribs even though they were bandaged with Kinesiology tape. It was cool though. Luke enjoyed and loved her. He often wondered why Zora would choose a scarred, desperate man over anyone with greater status. Luke believed at one point she worked for Ike, but he dismissed that thought based on his own beliefs. Zora genuinely loved Luke, and she had issues as well.

"Baby, if we're supposed to be together, why do you keep me in the dark. I understand where your coming from, but if my life is in danger as well, why don't I need to know?" Zora asked.

Luke thought she was asleep. He was caught off guard with her small intrusiveness, but he expected her curiosity, and Luke was prepared to handle it.

"Zora, hear me out baby. I don't think you really want to know what happened in Maryland, and since we're together, I could ruin your life if I told you. And to be real with you, I don't want to remember what happened there. The most important thing is that I'm alive and I got what I came for. I was almost murdered twice. That's all you need to know."

Zora heard closure in his voice and decided to drop it, but her guess was that he had killed someone. Whatever happened would remain a mystery to her. Since silence followed Luke's last statement, Zora saw it as an opportunity to come clean about her past.

"Luke, I've been so concerned about you and what you get into when you're not around me that I never fully came clean about myself."

Moonlight flooded the room, and Luke could see her eyes piercing a hole through his soul. Luke's mind scrambled, but it landed on his prior theory about her working for Ike. Luke never saw that look in her eye. He had a feeling she held out on some major shit.

"Me getting a job and moving to Connecticut is more complex than being grown and venturing out. It's much deeper than that."

Luke looked confused. "How deep is it?"

"Its deep baby. Its real deep."

Luke was so paranoid that he was prepared to knock her out if there was any association with Ike. He had no time for snakes.

"Baby, promise me that you won't judge me."

"Considering my circumstances, its hard for me to judge anyone at this point."

Luke broke away from her, and he lit the piff he toted on all night. His nerves were on fire as he braced for a bombshell.

"Remember I told you I moved up here because of my job?"

Luke nodded as he inhaled the greenery.

"That's not the only reason why I moved from New York."

Luke listened attentively. She was tight with her mother, father, and her first cousin Robbie. Zora was in a teenaged relationship with his best friend Hubert. She had a click she ran with, and Zora went through the normal motion of a teenager until her world was flipped upside down.

"Me, Hubert, and Robbie were in Hubert's apartment smoking and drinking. I went to the bathroom, came out, and finished off my beer. And then I started to get dizzy until I passed out. I woke up the next morning naked with Hubert and Robbie next to me. They were also naked. I had dried semen on my inner thigh. They drugged and raped me. Someone whose supposed to be my cousin and my boyfriend?" Zora broke down. Luke embraced her as she wept. Luke was horrified by what happened to her, but relieved that her major dilemma wasn't Ike related.

"Don't cry baby. I'm here now and would never let anything happen to you."

Luke gave her the opportunity to let it all out. She was scarred and traumatized from her past, but he still wasn't going to tell her about Maryland. After coming down from her emotional spurt, Luke wanted to hear the rest of the story.

"Zora, what happened to your cousin and boyfriend?"

She wiped her tears."My dad killed them."

"Huh?"

"And that's when the drama started. Everyone, including family, felt that it was consensual. My father going to prison for the rest of his natural life was the beginning of the end for me. Everybody thinks it's my fault that my father is a lifer, including my grandmother. My mother took me out of the Bronx and moved to Queens. My mother and me lived in Queens for ten years before I moved up here and met you. That's the story of my life."

Luke continued to hold Zora after she told him about her trauma. He looked at her no differently. Luke kissed her for confirmation. The love they felt for one another was surreal. With tears in her eyes, they continued to kiss passionately until Luke's main cell phone vibrated on the nightstand. He respectfully broke the embrace, and Luke tended to his phone. The call came from Maryland Correctional Institution for Women. Curiosity drove him to answer the call.

"This is a collect call from..."

"Talisha," she said when prompted.

"Will you accept?"

Luke knew Zora was ear hustling, but he wondered why the hell Talisha was locked up. He had to know what was situated in her mind. Thoughts of the murders soared throughout his brain. Luke felt like having a bowel movement.

"I'll accept."

And then silence developed between them. It had been three weeks since Luke spoke to Talisha. Luke took a deep breath, and he knew he had to watch what he said.

"I missed out on a gig because of you. Where the fuck is my safe?"

Talisha was bewildered. Luke didn't sound like he had a treasure stashed in the safe. Aside from being traumatized by the hardcore, scar faced butch females running the pre-sentence unit, Talisha felt stupid. She couldn't figure out an approach. Luke was way ahead in the game.

"Luke, I was going to pick the safe, take some cash, and replace it once I got back to Waterbury. My cousin owes me money anyway, and I was going to use that to pay you back."

Luke smirked as her lie seeped through her teeth. Despite the thorn she was in his side, Luke would never deny Baron a mother, but he could deny a placement in his heart. He hated her.

"So what are you doing calling collect from a Maryland jail?" Luke knew she got tangled with Omar, but to him, she wasn't a high priority. Luke had to get those greenbacks.

Talisha had a lie for the question she knew he would ask.

"Your brother's homeboy Omar and a few of his people approached me and my cousin and invited us to a get together. We got drunk and passed out, but cops raided his home and snatched all of us, but they wanted Omar for a murder in Waterbury. They found Timmy Blairwood's body and they think Omar had something to do with it."

Luke thought Timmy lived on borrowed time anyway, but Quincy worked in mysterious ways. He knew Barry, Omar's homeboy, had the murder weapon. After Quincy sent his people to him, Barry gave up the gun willingly, and he sold Omar out on his whereabouts. When Quincy dropped the proposition of planting the gun in Omar's house on Luke, Timmy's body lay dead in the woods.

When Talisha told Luke what she was being charged with, he knew she needed a great, expensive lawyer. A kilo and a gun in one's possession was a ticket to a lengthy stretch. Talisha deserved her sticky situation, but he knew the kilo and the gun belonged to Omar. Talisha was hood, but she didn't know anything about the game. Despite her lies running up the phone bill, and the hatred Luke had towards her, she was still Baron's mother.

"Look Talisha, I will do the best I can, but it's going to be a hot minute, and if by miracle I help you get out, stay the fuck away from us. Stealing from me is the worst thing you can do. You crossed the line with that shit. I could have been working right now."

Talisha wanted out of jail immediately, but she held her tongue because Luke was her only hope. She knew Luke was lying about what was inside the safe, but she decided to stick to playing his game. Talisha felt that Luke rode through four states, and took back what was rightfully his, but either way and at the moment, Talisha had her pussy to guard from the thirsty inmates.

"Baby, I want us to start over. I know I wronged you..."

Luke hung up. Talisha called, spread her lies, and heard what she wanted to hear. If she weren't Baron's mother, Luke would let the bitch rot. Zora felt Luke's bitterness after he abruptly ended the call and held him. She loved Luke, and would respect his wishes of not inquiring about Maryland. Zora turned over, snuggled her rear into his crotch, and fell asleep.

While Zora slept, Luke sat at the table and smoked another blunt to help him sleep. Now that Quincy's plan was in full effect, Luke had to focus on more lics, pay Ike the money, and avoid an early grave.

CHAPTER 30

A month later

THE FREEZING RAIN TICKLED Luke's windshield. It was painfully cold. Luke left the comfort of Zora's king-sized bed to look for lics. Time was dwindling, and Luke was strapped for it. He was four hundred thousand short of the one point five million dollars. Luke had to move fast. The first opportunity he got to rob and steal, Luke been on it. During the last two days, he'd begged Zora frantically to go back to New York until things died down, but she'd argued and refused. Zora's loyalty was high, but Luke didn't want to live with another regret if something happened to her. Regretful acts and deeds piled up, and Luke didn't want to place Zora in that category.

With the pain in his ribs subsiding, Luke was ready for some action. He was willing to lay his life on the line for his loved ones. He was focused, and his guard remained high. Luke hoped Wil had the heart to protect his family. He was the only man in Luke's corner. Without Wil, his family were sitting ducks. Wil was a former cop, but Ike and Toby were current killers.

Luke drove slowly and carefully through an iced, north end section of Waterbury. The streets were vacant, quiet, and possessed no signs of activity. He'd spent too much time in the hood since he'd been prowling, and Luke planned on taking his mission to West Hartford, a high-end city, despite the slippery roads. Luke strategized a bank robbery, but he needed more than a handwritten note or gun. The exit strategy Luke had in mind was cloudy and vague. He'd fuck around and get himself killed, or snatched by police. Either way, Luke needed the cash, and fear of death or jail wasn't gonna stop him from getting it. Only death or prison could put a wrench in Luke's plans.

Luke was still unsuccessful. He saw an armored truck, and he found himself tailing it, but memories of Dan changed his mind. Dan's laughter, character, and other fond memories flooded his mind until he heard the bullet roar out the chamber of a gun, and Dan's body being cut down. Luke pulled over on the side of the road and cried. Zora had tried to convince him that Dan's death was not his fault, but Luke didn't agree. Dan and Rosa planned the heist, but Dan wouldn't have participated if it weren't for Ike coming for Luke's throat.

After he wiped away the tears, Luke's phone vibrated. It was Quincy calling collect. He answered on the third ring.

"I'll accept."

Renee woke up when Wil left her side to buy a pack of cigarettes. Wil was gone for five minutes. She rose out of the bed, checked on Baron, and walked to the bathroom. While she used it, the nagging thought of her only surviving son being in trouble pestered her. Renee had a hunch that it was Talisha behind whatever ordeal Luke was involved in, but she wasn't sure. She recalled her son being with Dan during the last days of his life, and Renee wondered if Luke was involved in the botched heist. She hadn't seen him since Dan's funeral, and it wasn't like Luke to be distant. Since Dan's death, she feared for Luke's life, and Renee's fear kept her up most nights. Every time the newspaper or news mentions details of the heist, it made her nauseous. If Luke didn't have anything to hide, he would show his face, but he hadn't, and it drove Renee into a fear-ridden shell.

Lately, Renee had the same reoccurring dream about Steve, but she'd always forget what the dream was about. She felt that Steve spoke to her from his grave, but Renee couldn't figure out his message. She detected a huge change in Wil because for the last three weeks, he'd been weird and weary. He was due back in a few minutes, and Renee had plans of confronting him.

As she brushed her teeth, Renee heard Baron cry. Within several seconds, Baron's crying became worse and more frantic. After she finished up in the bathroom, she went into the kitchen to prep him a bottle. When Baron stopped crying, she rushed into her bedroom. Renee's body froze in mid-movement. Baron wasn't in his bassinet. Her mind was on full alert, and her heart rate increased tenfold. Renee looked out the window and didn't see Wil's car; instead, she saw a black van in the driveway. Renee gripped her face in shock and fear. Baron was too young to climb out of his bassinet by himself. She stepped back a few feet, still clutching her face until she backed into a short, frail masked man. The man covered her mouth with force and tried to sweep her off her feet, but Renee's adrenaline made her feisty. She swung wildly while he struggled to pick her up. Renee heard Baron scream while she fought for her life until a tall muscular masked gunman who held Baron walked into the room with fury. He held Baron against his chest with one hand, and a .38 in the other, and he planted the barrel of the gun on Baron's head.

"Bitch, I'll blow this baby's brains out if you don't cooperate. Walk!" The gunman's voice was deep, gruff, and deadly. Renee didn't recognize it. The threat ceased Renee's wild movement. She gazed at the masked man's beady eyes with hatred.

"What's this all about?" Renee asked.

"Money. Now walk before I cut this kid's glory," the gunman said coldly.

After the men placed Renee in restraints, the men escorted them to the van. Renee hoped to God that Wil would round the corner, but he didn't. No neighbor stood in her line of vision as the wind made the freezing rain shift direction. When the gunman opened the back door to the van, a Spanish girl Renee had never seen was hogtied and gagged with tape. She looked petrified. Tears and mucus stained her face. An unopened bag of Enfamil and bottled water sat in the corner of the van. The gunman placed his hand around Baron's mouth to avoid unnecessary attention, and hopped in the van. With no car seat for the baby, the gunman sat on the floor with Baron and watched the hostages. Renee burned inside, and she wished the men dead. As terrified as Renee was, she began to accept her possible fate. She had no idea what the men wanted from her and her grandson, but she knew Luke and Wil knew the answer.

NEXT OF KIN

When the van turned right off of Columbia Blvd, Wil pulled up, parked, and walked into the house.

Luke entered MacDougall-Walker Correctional Institution still baffled about Quincy's request to see him. He was added to Quincy's visiting list after Steve's death, but it was his first time seeing Quincy in prison. Luke hoped it wasn't murder related. Hearing the buzzers on the doors, radios, and shoes click clacking the floor disturbed him. If Luke got pinned for his crimes, he knew he'd be hearing that shit for the rest of his life. Quincy spoke calm, and with urgency on the phone. In spite of his reluctance to be in a prison, Luke wanted to know what Quincy had to say.

Luke walked by women, children, and men who visited their loved ones. He spotted Quincy sitting at a table in the corner. It had been a minute since he saw Steve's best friend and former crime partner. Quincy's dreadlocks extended to the small of his back. His dark skin was flawless. At thirty-one, there wasn't a hint of facial hair on Quincy's face. When he smiled at Luke, he revealed evenly spaced teeth, but his smile turned into a mask of confusion at the sight of Luke's face. Luke's face was healing, but the scars were still noticeable. Quincy stood up to greet and embrace Luke. Even though Quincy was an inch shorter than Luke, Quincy's muscles bulged under his brown inmate jumpsuit.

"Peace fam."

"Peace. Its been a minute since I seen you. I hope that appeal is still in the works," Luke said.

"You already know. No jail could hold your boy down, feel me?"

"I feel you."

The men sat down. Quincy looked hard at Luke, and could tell he was dealing with hardship. Quincy had known Luke for twenty years, and he couldn't imagine Luke living a life of crime.

"Everything straight?" Quincy probed.

Luke smirked at the question.

"No."

"All this time I thought you were walking the road less traveled bro. What's good?"

Luke sent an indifferent glance about the room. "Nothing is good right now. And with all due respect, can we cut a rain check on the formalities? What did you need to see me for? Time is money, and money is time."

Quincy took no offense to Luke's boldness, but he analyzed Luke. Quincy almost felt like he was talking to his brother. Steve was the most brutally honest dude he'd known. Luke's scarred face was a symbol of war. Quincy had a feeling he was responsible for Luke's sudden, dark journey, but he brushed it aside.

"Luke, that thing I asked you to do...you did it with ease, and you asked no questions. Hell bent on revenge? You fucked up on cash? You popo?"

Quincy peeped Luke while he pondered the question. Luke's innocence was lost. He looked paranoid and sketchy. Luke's aura looked dark. He resembled Steve during his last days of walking on the Earth's soil.

"Me, popo? No. Hell bent on revenge and being fucked up on money is an understatement."

Quincy raised an eyebrow.

"Understatement? How much did Steve's murder impact you fam?"

Quincy probed, and Luke didn't have time for it, but it was understood. Luke was thankful Quincy had no bad news for him.

"It hit me hard man, but I don't think you called me up here to talk about Steve. What's the deal?"

Quincy looked at Luke without blinking. "Steve is the deal."

Neither man spoke after Quincy's comment. Luke's curiosity peeked. The silence was so thick that one would think the place went mute. Luke didn't have a muster seed of a clue about what was about to spill from Quincy's mouth. When Quincy dropped his dreaded head between his arms and sighed, Luke knew he was gonna walk out of the prison a head case.

"I called you up here to feel you out. Everything went smoothly in Maryland because Omar is being extradited next week, but I don't understand how a Catholic school, non-crime committing dude can slide easily and handle some shit like that. What's the catch?"

138

NEXT OF KIN

Luke looked him squarely in his eyes.

"A price tag over my head, and every member in my family, that's the catch."

Quincy's facial expression didn't change. Guilt plagued his mind. He knew who placed the tag over Luke's head. Quincy knew the day would come before the madman cried revenge or payback.

Quincy shook his head. "Fucking Ike Collins."

Luke's jaw dropped.

Quincy continued. "That regal bastard is using you to pay back the money me and Steve robbed him for. That motherfucker."

Luke filled him in. Luke broke everything down from the beginning to Luke's current status. Quincy sighed, smacked the table, and shifted several times in his seat. Quincy's entire world crashed after he heard Luke's revelation. Luke's small, noticeable limp and his healing wounds were a dead giveaway. Quincy's muscle wouldn't have the heart to go after a man like Ike. Luke and his family were paying for Steve and Quincy's sins.

"Luke, you got every right to be mad, but Steve did that for you and Renee. He wanted you to go to school. He tried hard to keep you away from all this shit."

Frustration etched in Quincy's face because he knew exactly how dangerous Ike was. Ike would go to any extreme to prove a point. An alarming feeling overwhelmed Quincy to the point of nausea. He could only imagine what Luke had gone through since he received the threat of death for him and his family. Luke spoke of his dangerous mission with accurate and precise detail. After Luke provided the details of his ordeal, Quincy described how they robbed one of Ike's safe houses in Camden, New Jersey, and made off with life altering cash and drugs. Quincy told Luke that an NBA star's life was in danger because of the lift. Ike knew Steve and Quincy were the ones responsible, and planned on exterminating them. If Steve didn't get killed and Quincy incarcerated, they would had been plant food years ago. Steve was fortunate to leave the Earth before Ike made it happen. Quincy was cagey in prison because of the threat on his life.

The men took everything in. Their revelations were so thick that neither man heard the cacophony of voices that filled the visiting room. Quincy moved his face closer to Luke's to avoid ear hustlers.

"So you were the third man of that heist Dan and that white chick tried to pull off?"

Luke nodded.

"Fuck. Look man, the bricks Omar killed Steve for...probably five hundred thousand dollars worth," Quincy said.

"And I need one point five million," Luke countered.

"My point exactly."

Luke looked at Quincy incredulously.

"So Steve got a hidden stash?"

Quincy had an eerie look in his eyes. "It's out there bro, but peep it Luke. The first thing you need to do is get the fuck out of here, keep your family safe and under watch. Everybody I trust is locked up so there's no help. If I ask the niggas I know on the outside, they want details. This kind of shit can't get leaked."

Luke was convinced. If he could get a hold of the half of million, he can get Ike and Toby off his ass. Luke didn't need any more robberies, drug dealing, flipping, and killing. When Luke stood up to leave, Quincy embraced him. Devastated by Luke's news, Quincy watched Luke's back as he made his way out. Quincy wondered if today would be the last day he would see Luke alive. Ike was a killing machine, but Luke was like a raccoon that was trapped in a corner. When Quincy got back to his cell, he pulled out his prayer rug and asked Allah to guide Luke through the dark and dangerous future. If Luke killed Ike, Ike's sheep would scatter.

CHAPTER 31

Phoenix, Arizona

A LIGHT-SKINNED, BEAUTIFUL, thick brown-eyed groupie sucked NBA swingman Javon Wadsworth off in a limo while the driver headed to Javon's mini-mansion at five thirty in the morning. Weather forecasters promised a nice day. The woman looked so exotic and pure that Javon visualized her being the main lady in his life, but he destroyed that thought when he imagined the diversity of dicks the unknown woman may have had in her mouth. He'd be the laughing stock of the league, and Javon's image would be tarnished. Javon was versatile on the basketball court, and he multi-tasked in general. Widowed with two children, Javon spoke to his six-year-old in between moans and grunts as the beauty licked, gagged, and spat saliva on Javon's fuck stick. To the media and fans, Javon was a poor kid from Patterson, New Jersey, but to those who knew him well, he was a rich arrogant piece of shit who forgot where he came from.

Javon's thirst for women increased tenfold since his wife's body was found floating the Atlantic Ocean. The police still didn't have a suspect, and the fuzz fought tooth and nail to prevent the case from becoming cold. In a sick way, Javon secretly embraced it. Javon and his wife were together since high school, and their marriage was on the rocks. His wife threatened to take half of what he brought in. If Javon knew the factors that surround her death, he'd think otherwise.

Javon unloaded a glob of semen in her mouth as his body convulsed. The woman moved from her position, and spit his love juice into a napkin she retrieved from her purse.

"Shit, goddamn," Javon said like he ran a suicide drill. He slowly tucked his limp, empty penis back in his boxers, and pulled his pants up. The woman slid down the window and tossed his DNA. Exhausted, Javon cracked a smile while visualizing his bed. Since he didn't have practice in the afternoon, Javon wouldn't mind the company. She'd approached him at his teammate's party full of celebrities, athletes, and high profile politicians.

"You like?" The woman flipped her tits back into her bra.

"*Shit!* You already know, but check it; coach gave us the day off. We can take it back to the mansion, have a few drinks, smoke a little sour diesel, and fuck until the sun falls from the sky."

The woman chuckled. "That sounds good, but aren't you guys huge on drug testing?"

"There's always a way around that shit," Javon said. She moved in closer.

"So is that a yes?" Javon couldn't help himself. The chick was beautiful.

"No," she smiled.

Javon looked at her like she lost her mind. The bitch should be grateful a superstar of his status even glanced in her direction. In Javon's mind, he ruled everything around him because he had money.

"Don't be so uptight. I'm just playing baby, my God." She sucked softly on Javon's neck. She traced the outline of the dragon tattoo on his neck with her moist tongue, and she reached for his cock. Javon leaned back and relaxed. He didn't mind a second round of oral. Javon ran his large hands over his baldhead. His thick, dark eyebrows folded, his eyes were closed shut, and Javon's mouth was opened wide out of passion. Javon's dick nearly lost its erection when he felt something stick through the vein of his inner thigh. His passion filled face turned into a face of discomfort.

"Hold up," Javon said, interrupting the blowjob. "Something in this seat stuck me." His eyes scrambled for the foreign object.

She looked at Javon coldly.

NEXT OF KIN

"You mean this?" She held a syringe once filled with heroin that was now into Javon's bloodstream. Javon's face etched with confusion; he tried to figure out her motive. On cue, the woman tapped on the tinted privacy screen. When it slid open, Ike inched his manicured face in the opening.

"Surprise! If it isn't Mr. Slam Dunk. Since you'll soon be in an euphoric state, we'll be delighted to explain your post treatment plan once we near our destination."

Ike kept talking, but everything in sight, including Ike and the decoy, was a blur. Javon disregarded Ike, and fell into oblivion because the effect of the drug settled in. Javon felt at ease, relaxed, and fearless, for he thought he was dreaming, but Ike would never stand for any victim of his to die a painless death. Javon would feel the rug pulling from beneath his feet soon. Pressed for time, Ike ordered the driver to turn around, and head somewhere void and desolate.

Javon finally opened his eyes after his dope high, but soon wished he'd kept them closed. Ike and his female accomplice stood over him in the Sonoran Desert on top of the Santa Catalina Mountains. Javon's long arms and legs were bounded by gray duct tape. He was positioned on his side. Javon's mouth was free of restraint. If Javon screamed for help, his cry would only be heard by vultures, scorpions, armadillos, lizards, and endangered species. There wasn't a human being within a fifty-mile radius. Cacti and rare exotic plants surrounded his vision.

"I see you polished yourself quite well, but there is still a principle involved here..."

"Ike man, please. Don't do this bro. There wasn't nothing I could do about them up north niggas lifting the grip from the stash houses. Those other cats on your staff lost focus and slipped, but I was always on point."

Ike looked at the superstar flatly, and developed a rush seeing him in his predicament. The decoy looked at him and shook her head. She walked closer to Ike, held him, and tried to kiss him, but Ike turned away.

"Not until you clean and rinse your mouth." Ike moved his attention to the bounded superstar.

"I always knew you were a coward so you running was not a surprise. I got over that, but you crossed me Mr. Wadsworth."

"Bro, whatever you need, I got you. I'm good now!" Beads of sweat spilled down Javon's face. Tears and dirt stained his face. He made a feeble attempt to escape his restraints, but it was useless. Buzzards squawked in the horizon. Dressed in all black with a long sleeve shirt, Ike wore that hot shit to protect his flawless skin from the sun, but he also found it easier to conceal his weapon.

"Steve is dead and Quincy is incarcerated. No longer a concern of mine. But when I find a way, that dreaded fool will die before he reaches a decade in that cage, but as for you, it's a little more personal. Police, citizens, and Sherlock Holmes don't know who killed your wife, but I do. I fucked her and her friend and had them killed. I made your wife neighbors with the Titanic."

Shock, anger, and an overwhelming feeling shot through Javon's bounded body, but there was nothing he could do about it. The only thing he could do was beg for his glamorous life.

"You killed my wife! We even bro! What the fuck? I was going to give you a lump sum man! Come on!"

Ike pulled out a Desert Eagle, and he trained it on Javon's head.

"Ludicrous. You hated your wife. I want your life," Ike said gravely.

"Ike, please man!" Javon cried like he was a second removed from the womb. Javon was so scared that he pissed and shitted himself. Ike looked at him, and couldn't wait to send him on his way.

"You always said you'd be king one day whether it was dethroning me, or being who you are today. And you know what? You are a king in your own right. You're a rose that grew from concrete, but kings lack the caution of a common man. You told on me Javon. You participated in the plan to destroy my life. You went to college, and made it to the league with flying colors and didn't look back. But I defeated the case. You thought I was finished like my father. I have paperwork with *your* signature. Two life sentences they could have given me after I groomed you. The world knows you as the next thing coming, but they don't see your whiskers. You're a rat, and I'm going to make sure you die like one."

"I recanted the statement, and you know that! I think I'm entitled to the benefit of the doubt Ike! Jesus Christ man, please!"

Ike shot Javon a venomous look. "And you're also entitled to a bullet."

Ike fired the cannon and landed a bead on Javon's head. Blood spilled from his brain as Ike and the bitch admired the leaking NBA body like it was one of Leonardo Da Vinci's paintings. *Sports Center* would air a segment on the life of Javon Wadsworth.

After the limo driver drove the odd couple out of the desert, Ike's cell phone rang and he answered.

"It's done. We got 'em. All three are in motion now," one of Ike's paid goons stated.

"Good. Keep them safe until I return. Don't inflict any harm or punishment on them unless you want to be the newest corpse inside the showroom."

"Absolutely not," Ike's inferior said seriously.

Ike hit the end button, and he sped dialed Toby.

"Yeah boss?" Toby answered.

"Mr. Law will up the ante on his crime spree. You will assist when necessary. I don't care if its White House related. Understood?"

"I'm on it boss."

Once Ike disconnected the call, he leaned back, unzipped his pants, and beckoned the decoy to suck his dick. He closed his eyes and smiled as she wrapped her thin lips over his meaty cock. Life was good for Ike.

CHAPTER 32

"Zora." Silence.

"Zora!" More silence. Luke plugged his dead phone into the wall, and continued to call for her. Luke knew she'd taken the day off, and he figured she'd gone to the grocery store. He plopped onto her bed, closed his eyes, and thought of the possibilities where Steve may had hidden his share of the heist. As soon as Luke's phone rang, he picked it up prematurely. The detective's voice made him grit his teeth.

"Luke, we need to have a talk at the station. No one is pointing fingers, but we need to solve this investigation and move on with our lives. Is four-thirty good for you?"

Luke looked at his phone incredulously.

"Four-thirty ain't good detective or any other time. Tired of y'all motherfuckers harassing me about this group home bullshit! What the fuck?"

"The profanity isn't necessary, and it will be in your best interest to control your tone." The detective was losing patience with Luke's lack of corporation. "And if you didn't do anything, what is there to worry about? I'm just asking for your full cooperation so we can proceed. The hostility is getting you nowhere."

"Well, you need to go somewhere else with it then. A motherfucker dies in a group home, but you make me feel like a fucking suspect so fuck all your therapeutic approach bullshit."

"Once again, control the tone and bring your ass down here before I send a cruiser. Is that direct enough for ya?"

"Eat a dick." Luke ended the call, and tossed his phone on the bed.

The chime of his voicemail grabbed Luke's attention. Luke checked his phone, and it read that he had thirty new voice messages from Wil. Fear gripped Luke by the neck. Wil would not call thirty times if everything were fine. After he heard the panic in Wil's voicemail, Luke dropped the phone, held his mouth open, and clawed at his face in agony. Flooded with despair and horror, he collapsed to the floor and screamed. He banged and clawed at the carpet. The pain and misery Luke felt was indescribable. Flashbacks of the day Steve was buried, the first time Luke got kidnapped, unburied bodies, group home burglaries, robberies, Dan's death, murders, the few attempts on his life, Talisha's betrayal, the group home death, Omar, Quincy's revelations, the head of a corpse, and his family's kidnapping gnawed at Luke's sanity.

Despite everything, Luke got a grip. He began to gather his strength. The frantic knocking on the door startled him, and he drew his weapon. Luke pointed it at the door, and walked to it slowly and with caution.

"Luke, Zora, its Wil! Open up man!" Wil sounded like someone was after him. Luke lowered his weapon, and he opened the door. He grabbed Wil with his free hand, shoved him against the wall, and trained the gun on Wil's upper body.

"You let this happen! This is your fault motherfucker!" Luke's war-ridden face, and the coldness of Luke's eyes scared the shit out of Wil. Luke was a man apart, and not in the right state of mind. He was dangerous.

"Luke, I was gone for ten minutes man. It is my fault, but please, put the gun down. This is some fucked up shit, but you killing me is not going to bring the family back," Will pleaded.

Luke was unsteady, and his arm shook while he held the gun. The tip of his finger touched the trigger as he shot daggers at Wil. Common sense drove Luke to put the gun down. Luke broke down, and he had a weeping session. Wil held him to help ease the pain. He was just as fucked up as Luke. Wil loved Renee, and treated Baron like a grandson.

It hit Luke like a bag of bricks. He was so engulfed in his emotions that he didn't think about Zora. Luke charged over to the bed, scooped his phone, and dialed her number. He heard the ringtone of her phone under her side of the bed.

"They got Zora too."

"Goddamit!" Wil roared.

Luke's phone rang. The number was blocked. He looked at Wil for verification. Luke touched the answer key on his phone, put the phone on speaker, and said nothing.

Ike said, "I know you're there Mr. Law. If wise, you'll listen carefully. A single cent short of my coin will result in a blood bath for your family...in case your wondering where their at. They're safe...for now. You have ninety-six hours to show and prove. I will leave you a number. Once my coin is collected, you dial the number I will provide for you, let it ring twice, hang up, and my staff will give you a meeting point. Remember, no stupid monkey business. My faculty carries the tools of immediate death. Is that clear Mr. Law?"

"Loud and clear," Luke said with a hostile face.

"Good. Toby will be there to assist if necessary."

Ike ended the call as soon as he gave Luke the number.

Boiling with fury, Luke ground his teeth and clenched his jaw tight. "Wil, I'm telling you this right now, I don't need four days. I'm getting them back tonight! If you don't want to ride this out with me, its all good, but either way, I'm killing that motherfucker!"

Wil looked at Luke calmly.

"I'm riding with you, but not until we spend a little time in the war room."

"Wil man..."

"Hold up and hear me out Luke. We are on the same page on everything at his point, even if we have to kill a host of motherfuckers to get them back, but the direction you want to go in was created out of bad energy, and its only a recipe for death. Right now, we don't know what we're dealing with, but every strong force has a weakness."

Luke listened attentively while Wil provided a possible blueprint to get Renee, Baron, and Zora back. Wil's experience as a cop, and his appreciation for Napoleon made Luke think outside the box. The men exchanged more ideas, wrote down what Luke knew about Ike, jotted what Quincy knew about him, and traded scenario after scenario.

An hour later, as expected, Toby pulled up in front of Zora's building. Luke looked at him from the window, and developed an urge to cut Toby's throat, but Wil had a better plan.

"Did he see you when you came over here?" Luke asked.

"I doubt it. I would have noticed an all black tinted truck tailing me. You know where I live, right?"

"Mark Lane?"

"Yeah." Wil told him the apartment number, and handed Luke the key.

"Go upstairs in the apartment, go into the second room upstairs, and in the closet, there are two crates of weapons and a few vests. We'll be needing those." Wil took another look outside at the hideous bastard. "And don't forgot the binoculars. You may have to dig for them, but they are in the closet."

Luke nodded. The less Ike and Toby knew about Wil, the safer they were. After he heard a few more details, Luke walked out the front door of Zora's building. Toby shot his dark, beady eyes at Luke and cracked an evil, sinister smile. Luke returned an icy glare of his own, and he shifted his attention on his car. Toby started the truck and waited for Luke to pass him. Once Luke was in motion, Toby trailed him to Wil's apartment. Once there, Luke stepped out of his car bombarded with anger, fear, and uncertainty, but his confidence was high. The second Toby slips, he would never stand up again. With that in mind, Luke made moves inside Wil's apartment, and tackled phase one of the mission.

CHAPTER 33

Outskirts of New Jersey

Crickets moaned throughout the night. The heavy glare of the moon had the capability of exposing those who chose to remain hidden. Two heavily armed guards were posted in front of the secluded safe house on the outskirts of New Jersey. Steve and Quincy schemed from a vantage point in the woods. The men were strapped, and ready to rob the safe house once the right moment fell into place. No dialogue was exchanged as Steve and Quincy plotted on the guard's weaknesses. Two hours had passed since the third and fourth guard slid out. Now it was only two of them who guarded the jackpot. Steve and Quincy waited patiently in the cold, dark wooded area that surrounded the house. Steve frequented the house, peeped the routine, the drug factory, and the blind spots not captured on camera. Javon Wadsworth, one of the patrolling guards, went in and out of the house. Quincy thought highly of Javon because of his basketball talent, but the fortune in that safe house erased any high regard Quincy had for him.

"We need to hit these niggas before anyone makes a surprise visit," Quincy said, breaking the long-lived silence.

"Be patient fam. I know this shit like clockwork. If we hit these niggas now, we'll be going away with half. That fat nigga Walker supposed to be making another drop off any minute now with another load fresh from the jet." Steve went into his bag and pulled out a sniper rifle, and planted the base of it on a large rock.

Quincy tensed. "Steve, you sure this is the day of the shipment? You think niggas actually chop shit up in that house?" Quincy had many lingering doubts. It was hard to imagine that kind of import being guarded and packaged in the woods.

150

NEXT OF KIN

"*Ike never has anything short of that out here,*" *Steve said confidently.* "*The house is small, but the compartment leading underground is where the wealth is. I was down there, trust me.*"

"*Steve man...*"

Steve waved off Quincy's words. "*Look, we risking our lives thinking small Quincy. Fucking small time. Tired of that shit. Fuck Ike and them goddamn bodies. That nigga don't put no fear in my heart.*"

"*He got a collection of cadavers in one of his gutted spots. That don't make you a little uncomfortable?*" *Steve ran his hand through his dreads.*

"*It did, but we talkin' life changin' cheddar. I treat this shit like stocks; the higher the stock, the greater the reward. I'm not willing to spill an opportunity because the motherfucker showed us some decaying bodies. Them dead niggas was scared of him; I'm not. He tryin' to pull scare tactics to keep niggas like us away from his money. Fuck that professor talkin' son of a bitch,*" *Steve said. Steve had no fear in Ike, and vowed to murder him if Ike ever came after him.*

Quincy had a bad feeling about the heist. It seemed too easy. His first instinct told him he should prevent the robbery, but a come-up was too enticing. Besides, Steve's mind was locked. Since the silence set in, Quincy seized the opportunity to release his nagging thoughts.

"*Steve, it took you a week to stake this shit out?*"

"*Two. My hotel bill was crazy staying all them days down here.*" *Steve screwed and attached the loose ends on the rifle.*

"*I know you don't fear Ike, but I think you sleepin' on him. That dude is an evil genius, and I have a feeling he may be ahead of us.*"

Steve worked on the rifle while he pondered Quincy's words.

"*Why you say that?*"

"*I don't know, but I have a feeling he knows more than we think,*" *Quincy said.*

Steve adjusted the rifle some more and stood up.

"*We supposed to stop this shit because you think you saw that big motherfucker that's always with Ike? Come on man, Ike is more than likely hated and wanted dead by many. He ain't leaving Ike's side to tail two out of towners. We almost four hours from CT. You was amped up about this shit, drove down here to meet me for the biggest lic of our lives, and now you acting suspect.*" *Steve looked Quincy squarely in his eyes.* "*If you want out, go wait in the car.*"

"*It ain't like that Steve.*"

"*Right now, we doing the work in between a want and a goal. Motherfuckers have that desire and goal, but never want to press the action in the middle. Omar kick that takeover shit, and does nothing about it. Timmy too. Them niggas are dummies that want to party and bullshit. Why do you think I don't fuck with them when it comes to anything major? Because they ain't focused and lack discipline...*"

The headlights stopped their conversation in mid-sentence. Steve looked through the scope of the rifle to get a better look. Quincy looked on with binoculars. The driver of a commercial truck proceeded slowly on the rough terrain until he came to a stop adjacent to the safe house. A short, pudgy, South American man stepped out of the truck. When the truck driver opened the trailer, the three men guarding the safe house walked inside of it. Steve knew the coke was drilled into the walls of the trailer. The longer Ike's men took drilling it out, the bigger the take. Forty-five minutes later, the men walked out the trailer carrying seven duffle cargo bags, and brought them inside the house.

Steve remained at his post behind the sniper rifle, modified the scope, and wondered if someone else was inside the house other than the guard Javon shared the shift with. The driver walked out followed by Javon with a duffle bag full of payment in his hand. The driver lit a cigarette, shared a little dialogue, and took off. Javon remained outside and on guard. Steve killed a little time so the men could get smug.

Quincy followed the blind spots that lead up to the safe house. He moved quietly and cautiously. Small piles of rocks that Steve set up when he staked the place labeled the blind spots. The bad feelings Quincy had about the lift subsided, but caution remained in his back pocket. As Quincy got closer to the house, the goons' voices became more detailed and clear. The gut feeling Quincy had remained, but there was no turning back. He was too close to the treasure to catch cold feet. Quincy looked in the woods and his eyes searched for Steve, but he wasn't visible; trees and bushes surrounded and concealed Steve's vantage point. Quincy knew the plan inside and out, but he still thought it was too good to be true. He was literally a few thousand feet away from the obstacle and the prize. Left over thoughts about the hit went out the door. It was time to make moves. After slowly counting a five count backwards, Quincy took a deep breath and made his appearance.

"*No need to state the obvious.*"

Javon knew exactly what it was, and he had a strong idea who was behind the mask, but cooperation was the only idea he could muster. Javon promised himself that if he lived through the masked man's ambush, he would disappear. There was over a million dollars worth of cocaine in the house. With that gone, Ike would have

NEXT OF KIN

Javon dead within a week. Ike had killed for less. Javon's fate depended on Eddie's arrival. If Eddie were on his job, he'd be on his way out of the house to shoot the armed masked man. Javon was sure surveillance covered the perimeter.

"Uggghhh!" a wounded man yelled.

Steve aimed for a leg, but he accidentally shattered the man's spine when the man attempted to rescue Javon from gunpoint. "I'm hit son! I can't feel my legs man! Fuck! I'm hit!"

Moments later, the cook ran out the front door hurriedly, but a set of bullets cut him down. Steve emerged from the dark after he gunned down the cook, and threatened to bring death on the wounded man if he didn't shut the fuck up. Steve walked up to Javon, struck him in his face with the handle of the sniper rifle, and trained it on him.

"I could shoot a lot better from up close."

Javon looked at his friend's corpse bleeding out in the dirt. Javon heard Eddie's grunts, but couldn't see him. Javon wasn't a dummy; he left his mouth pursed. The first shift guards weren't due until seven, and sunrise wasn't happening anytime soon. A million thoughts danced in Javon's head as he pictured his NBA dreams being wiped away with a wave of Ike's hand. The masked men now had access to over a million dollars worth of coke. It was difficult for a man like Ike to digest a petty theft, never mind a million and a half large. If Ike were coming for Javon's throat over the robbery, then Javon would make sure Ike would never see the streets again. Javon knew the suits were building a case against Ike, and Javon also knew his testimony could land Ike in the shit hole for the rest of his natural life.

"I'll tell y'all where it's at; that's not a problem. Just don't kill me...please," Javon pleaded.

Javon knew it was those Connecticut cats, but it didn't matter. If Javon didn't execute an escape plan fast, it would be his own blood leaking all over the place.

"Get up and give 'em the car keys."

Javon complied, and he handed Quincy the keys.

"Go get the truck. By the time you come back, the bricks will be ready to be loaded," Steve instructed.

Quincy nodded, hopped in Javon's car, and sped off. Steve kept the barrel of the sniper rifle pointed at Javon's head when they walked in the door. No one else was inside. A mountain sized portion of cocaine stood on the table. Since the cook died protecting it, Steve ordered Javon to bag the drugs, and for Javon to lead Steve to the underground where Ike's goons cooked the hard white. Steve smirked

153

underneath his mask. He knew it was worth the trouble. Steve ordered Javon to transport all that shit outside with the nose of his rifle.

After he clearedout the safe house, Quincy arrived with the truck. Since time was sensitive, the men didn't have time to drill off the wall panels to stash the coke. Instead, the men stashed seventy-five kilos within the debris and clutter of the truck. It was a huge and necessary risk, but it was worth the reward once Steve and Quincy touched ground in Waterbury.

An hour later, Javon fought his way out of his restraints. Since he only worked with Eddie, and never considered Eddie a friend, he left him exactly where he dropped after being shot. A week after the hit, police snatched Ike. While Ike was in custody, Javon decided to cooperate from the outside, and threw more wood into the flames when he connected Ike to two bodies to ensure his own safety after he lost a million dollars worth of Ike's drugs.

After making bail and fighting the case for a year, Ike beat the charges, and vowed to kill Javon if he ever came across him.

Quincy took off his bifocals after he read an article about Javon's mysterious disappearance. It was too early to assume death, but Quincy knew the basketball star's body was in some abandoned location being picked at by insects and animals. If Steve and Quincy never robbed the safe house, Javon would have participated in the ESPN top ten plays. Quincy refused chow, got comfortable on his bed, and worried about Luke until the lights went out.

CHAPTER 34

THE INHUMANE CONDITIONS of the barn were the least of Renee and Zora's worries as their minds were sunken deep with uncertainty. The horrific conditions of the barn could kill animals. It was so cold in there that the women's hands and feet were numb, but fear disabled them from feeling pain. Death seemed inevitable. Renee and Zora were bounded and scared. Their mouths were covered with duct tape, but they spoke volumes with their eyes. One of the guards had his eye on Zora, and couldn't wait for the opportunity to present itself for him to have his way with her.

Zora was more frightened than Renee. Renee's conscious was numb, and she was willing to sacrifice her own life to save Luke, Zora, and Baron from slaughter once they took Baron away. Renee was tired of trying to figure out everything, and where everything fell into place. She had no idea what was going on, but Renee had a deal in place once she found out the reasoning for their predicament.

Renee looked at Zora apologetically. She knew the woman was in love with Luke for her to share the same fate, but Renee cursed Luke for not preventing her involvement. She factored in Talisha, and the role she probably played in their kidnapping. Either way, Renee would find out soon enough.

Luke's words replayed in Zora's head. He told her to leave, and to stay put until the dust settled, but Zora's heart won over her mind. Instead of regretting her decision to stay with Luke, she was chilled by what she believed was the inevitability of her death. Zora prayed to

God for redemption since being snatched out of her apartment. She thought of her mother. Time lapsed since Zora's last conversation with her; she hoped her mother didn't try calling. Zora knew her mother would worry if she were unable to reach her. She could do nothing more other than pray, cry, and remain scared.

The muscle bound light-skinned guard unlocked the door and walked in. The grotesque scar on his cheekbone was frightening. His eyes were set on Zora, and the man's eyes spelled rape. He was the masked man who put the gun to Baron's face at the house. He knelt next to Zora, forcefully grabbed her hair, and licked the side of her face. Zora's eyes were closed tight, but the tears still spilled from the violation. The muscled goon's breathing got heavier. He couldn't help himself. Renee watched from her restraint on the folding chair consumed with anger. The guard slid his hand underneath Zora's bra, and he cupped her breast. The pervert unzipped his pants with his free hand, and he began to masturbate. Zora made all the noise she could with the gag on her mouth. She tried to use the little strength she had to turn away from him, but it was useless. The man was too strong and too high on lust to let up. The man unbuttoned her jeans and pulled them down halfway, but his partner's voice threw a wrench in his plan.

"Ike is here! Goddamn man, you going to fuck around and get yourself killed!" His rail thin partner looked at him disgustedly.

The man's erection was lost at the mention of Ike's name. He pulled her jeans up, and fastened them before pulling up his own. Ike appeared in the doorway seconds later with the decoy he used to murder Javon Wadsworth.

"Greetings." Ike looked at the hostages. "Remove the tape and take them to the bathroom," he ordered. The men removed the tape, restraint, and Vanessa, walked them to the bathroom.

Minutes later, Vanessa returned the women. The attempted rapist had Zora over his shoulder before laying her back down. Ike looked at Renee flatly, and he knew hundreds of questions brewed in her head.

"Ms. Law, I'm Ike. I'm sorry to meet you under this grave circumstance, but I want to ensure you that it's nothing personal. I just want what is owed to me."

Confusion covered Renee's face.

"So you have us kidnapped?"

NEXT OF KIN

"Your son owes me one point five million," Ike said.

"Do you expect me to believe my son owes you that kind of money? Luke could barely stand on two feet. That's absurd."

Ike chuckled. "Luke huh? Why don't you try the son before him?"

Zora kept her mouth closed, but her ears and eyes were open. Luke's description of Ike was accurate; he was calm, collected, and evil. Zora was petrified, and she wondered if Luke would come through for them. The second she was snatched from her apartment, Luke's revelation was on the money, but now, she was about to hear the other side of the story. She saw the anger flash through Renee's eyes.

"Steven has been dead for six years! What the *fuck* does he have to do with any of this?" Renee asked belligerently.

"Everything. On March eighth, six years ago, an associate of mine who is no longer breathing introduced us. I liked Steven because he was brilliant. I needed him. Connecticut was a gold mine, and I needed someone I *trusted* to have it circulate a hundred fold, but my first instinct told me something was off about your son...so I put a tail on him and his partner Quincy. I had them followed for months. Whenever they picked up shipments, I would send someone to follow them back to Connecticut, but Steve and Quincy earned my trust so I stopped tailing them. Big typo in my line of work."

Renee trembled, cried, and looked at Ike scornfully.

"So you killed him?"

"No, Ms. Law, I played no role in your son's death; however, I wished I had. Grand piracy is sudden death."

Anger churned in Renee's chest. "You are a very sick man."

"My God, I know, and I'm sick to the point where I'll cut your tongue out of your mouth if you say that again, so please Ms. Law, abide by that or you'll force my hand." After Ike's threat, he told the men to tie the women back up.

"On November thirteenth of that year, two of my men were shot; one of them got expired, and one of them fled from the safe house. Your son's antics cost me one point five million and three men. One of them will never walk again. Coincidentally, karma hunted Steven and Quincy down and caught them. That great feeling about your son's demise and Quincy's incarceration was a teaser, but I'm still down one point five million. Your thieving son and his crime partner drove out of *my* state with seventy five kilos of cocaine valued at twenty grand per!" Ike was revved up.

Renee knew the man meant serious business. She needed to eliminate her worry about everyone's pending death, and structure a strategy of getting this man back his money.

"Luke is aware of the mass disappearance. Ms. Law, Zora, to add a little relief, he probably isn't too far away from having my coin. If the heist of that money truck were successful, you would've been safe and sound in Connecticut, but he's making money in more ways than one. I will kill you all if he isn't here with my coin by Saturday. And I have flesh-eating dogs that would love to feast on Baron. I'm pretty sure his skin is pure." Ike stopped mid sentence, paced in the close quarters, and stopped in front of them.

"His ex-girlfriend," Ike paused, looked at Zora, and exposed his villain smile, "ran away with his safe. Luke traveled a lot of ground to get it back...and he did. I saw it all from the comfort of my mansion, right from my computer. He drove all the way to Maryland to retrieve what he took and robbed for. Unfortunately, my tracking device couldn't capture what went on behind closed doors, but I had an idea and its concrete."

Ike fished for a piece of paper, and he tossed Renee a folded online article that was a replica from the *Gazette* newspaper in Maryland. Omar and Talisha's grim faced mug shots and their crimes appeared below them. The paper also described three deaths in a Maryland suburb. Talisha was being charged with drug and gun possession. Renee was furious and wasn't surprised at Talisha for being a slut, but she knew the drugs and money belonged to Omar. Renee cared for and accepted Omar over the years, but she never liked him around Steve, and was always wary of him.

"Luke was in both of those locations," Ike continued. "I saw him run like a bat out of hell after killing the men, but most importantly, he retrieved my coin without incident. Two days later, his ex and her new lover made the paper. Luke not killing Omar for bedding his girlfriend is far beyond me, but I know nothing of their business. Prince George County and the rest of the world don't know who plucked those three men off the earth except for me. For Mr. Law to go through such extremities to collect my coin, your lives may be spared, but don't ever keep hope up."

NEXT OF KIN

Zora's eyes got wide. The information Luke didn't want to tell her filled her ears. It sounded accurate because she picked him up from Maryland, and his body was beaten and wounded. Zora couldn't blame Luke for not wanting to reveal his horrific, necessary crimes.

Renee wasn't sure how much more revelation she could take. She could kill Talisha at that point. Luke had never been in trouble with anyone, but Luke jeopardized his freedom and livelihood to keep everyone alive. That explained Luke's distance after the botched armored truck robbery. His battle-filled face revealed all. Luke was on a crime spree, and Dan was killed while he helped him.

Ike took out his cell phone, and pulled up a video of Steve in action. He placed the phone in front of the women so they could watch. Three minutes into the footage, Renee felt nauseous. With her own eyes, including Zora's, they watched an unmasked Steve use a sniper rifle to shatter a spine, and end a life. Renee turned away from the truth. Ike stopped the footage.

Ike said, "Steve labeled all the blind spots on the perimeter, but he moved from his vantage point and accidently slid outside of the blind spot."

Renee could say no more. The proof was in the pudding, but Steve was still her son, and it wouldn't matter if he injured or murdered someone. It took Steve's death to know what kind of monster he really was, but she would always love him. Renee looked at Ike squarely, and came to a decision.

"Ike, I have six hundred thousand dollars in retirement..."

"One point five million dollars, and not a cent short of it."

Ike put his phone away, ordered his guards to stay alert, and proceeded to leave. The frail guard attempted to reseal Renee's mouth until she jerked her head away.

"Ike."

Ike stopped his travel, and he turned to face her.

"Yes."

"Can you order him to keep his hands off of my son's girlfriend? If you didn't show up, he would've raped her."

159

Ike looked at the muscle bound fuck coldly. Perspiration set in on the big guy. He was in a world of shit. Ike was a murdering motherfucker, but he despised rapists.

"Ike man, come on. These bitches is scared. I would nev..."

Ike drew a cannon, fired it, and put a gaping hole in his employee's head. The loud sound scared the women, and the shooting left them in a state of shock. Ike casually slid his weapon back in his holster, and walked away as if he stepped on a roach.

The women were fear stricken, and would've held on to each other if they weren't bound. The sight of the body posed as a great deterrent for any ideas of escape. Zora closed her eyes and prayed for a miracle while Renee realized that Ike had no conscience. He was a psychopath. The women hoped Luke could use his survival instincts and save them, but everything now was in God's hands.

After Ike and Vanessa departed, the frail guard continued his tight watch of the women. He looked at his fallen partner and shook his head. *He wouldn't be the first employee Ike murdered, and he damn sure wouldn't be the last."*

CHAPTER 35

TOBY GRITTED HIS TEETH as he thought of Ike's insults. Toby worked for the man for ten years, and wondered how he'd put up with such abuse for so long. If Ike weren't his bread and butter, Toby would had slit his throat a long time ago. Toby had numerous opportunities to put Ike to sleep, but he couldn't get the cash Ike was giving him from anywhere else. He hated Ike, but killing him would be like throwing cash out the window. Toby fumed because he had to deal with his bullshit. Having a seventh grade education had its disadvantages. The only thing Toby excelled at was murder and taking orders.

The anger transferred onto Luke. He wanted to dump a chamber of bullets in Luke's face, but he stuck to Ike's rules. Luke had two days to get that money. Toby doubted he had it in him to get the rest of the cash. Toby's horrid frown turned into a grotesque smile as thoughts of murder dominated the rest of his insignificant, meaningless thoughts. Toby hated that Luke showed him up in front of Ike, and Toby wanted Luke to die for it.

Toby grabbed the white cloth next to him, and he wiped the sweat off his forehead. Twenty-four-hour stakeouts could drain a man, especially one that weighed over three hundred pounds. Toby tucked the cloth into his pocket, grabbed his gun, got out of the truck, exhaled the cigar smoke into the frosty night, and snuck over to the side of Luke's three family residence to go take a piss. Relief set in once his urine touched the ground. Thoughts of blood spilling made noise in his head while Toby drained his dick of the last two drops. All it would take was one phone call to turn Luke into plant food, but he knew that wasn't happening until the next two days. After he tucked in his limp penis, Toby looked up on the third floor living room window, and he saw a shadowy figure behind a curtain. He assumed it was zooming in on him. Toby pointed his Glock at the window, and marked the shape behind the curtain. He tucked the gun away, died his cigar, and headed back to his truck.

Toby started the engine, and heat wafted out of the radiator. He laughed at his foolish thoughts of slaying his boss. Without Ike, he'd be an indigent who crawled around for scraps. Toby thought about the lump sum Ike was gonna pay him once Luke stopped breathing, and it called for a celebration. Toby fished in his breast pocket, and he pulled out a *Cohiba Esplendido* cigar. He moved miscellaneous items to the side and looked for his lighter with his beefy hand. When Toby turned on the interior light, he shot a glance in the rearview mirror and almost had a heart attack. Luke was seated in the back seat holding a grim, scarred face and a thirty-eight.

"Looking for this?" Luke flicked the lighter twice.

Toby was alarmed, but he remained poised. He wondered how in the fuck Luke got into the truck, but investigations were useless. A vengeful man out for blood sat behind Toby with a gun pointed at him.

"You don't want to do this Luke. You heading into the wrong direction," Toby said with a dead calm.

"I think I'm headed in the right direction," Luke challenged.

Toby was too fat to make any sudden moves. His next thought was interrupted by Wil's entry from the passenger side door with a sawed-off shotgun trained at his face. Toby swallowed hard, and knew he was outmanned.

"What the fuck is this?" Toby asked, shocked that he was on the other side of the gun.

Luke took his gun by the barrel, swung it, and struck him on the side of his face. Blood streamed from his nose and mouth.

"What the fuck do you think this is? Where the fuck is my family?"

Toby spat blood out of his mouth onto the floor of the truck.

"I don't think you want to do that. He too strong for y'all. Fuckin' amateurs going to war with a specialist. You won't even reach him," Toby said, still remaining calm despite two guns pointed at him.

Wil inched his face close to Toby's. "This GPS would. And we are only going to ask you once. Where are they on this navi?"

Toby sighed and knew he was a done deal. He told them the exact location of where the family was being kept. Once Wil set the location, the men assisted Toby at gunpoint in the back of the truck. Wil handcuffed Toby, and placed a restraint on his legs. After the men got their hostage settled in his restraint, Luke and Wil decided to make the ride to New Jersey using Toby's truck since it was eleven o'clock at night, and the windows were tinted. Using a vehicle outside of Ike's circle of killers would prove fatal. Wil volunteered to drive because of Luke's state of mind. The men knew Toby was right about Ike's strength and power, but Luke and Wil had their backs against the wall. They were gonna either go into battle and rescue the family, or not come out of the battle at all.

Elizabeth cruised the mansion with her hoveround and barked petty orders to her men. They hated the old, evil bitch, but they never shared their mutual feelings out of fear of Ike. The guards provided top-notch security, and they would dismantle any threat that try to lay hands or guns on the Collins. They were paid well, but never felt appreciated. Elizabeth treated the dogs with more respect than any human being that was not a Collins.

Elizabeth moved to the room where Baron slept. Elizabeth looked down at the gentle soul, and she frowned. The baby was cute, but business was business. In Bruno's heyday, he inflicted bodily harm and death for those that stole from him, but Elizabeth understood and felt it was necessary. Every employee of the Collins understood the consequences, and they loved their families too much to try anything stupid. Ike and Elizabeth's continuing criminal enterprise remained strong despite everyone's hatred toward their bosses. Money kept the Collins away from death. Bruno was dead, but his protocol for piracy lived on. Adversaries took heed to the Collins' style of corporal punishment. Luke may not have killed and took the drugs, but association always bred similarity. Betrayal and thievery would never go unnoticed, even if it took an enemy's next of kin to fix it.

Baron woke up and started to cry hysterically. The baby's noise bothered her. Elizabeth had an urge to strike it. The baby's eyes bulged with fear and confusion. Her aged, wrinkled, tight-lipped, blue-eyed face scared him. She felt no love or compassion for the child. Baron was leverage and nothing more. Elizabeth maneuvered her chair outside the room while Baron wept. She called for Luz. She ran to Elizabeth's side in a matter of seconds.

"Quiet this thing. Ike is asleep. Where the fuck were you anyway?" Elizabeth looked at her like she was a piece of shit.

"I...I..."

"Never mind. You stay put with that kid. The little shit has been shouting all night. I *better* not hear it again for the rest of the night. Understood?"

"Understood," Luz replied obediently.

Luz watched Elizabeth stroll in that Hoveround without a care in the world, and Elizabeth resumed her tour of her own mansion.

Luz made Baron feel at ease in her arms. She fixed a bottle, sang, fed, and held Baron until he fell asleep. Luz found it odd that the Collins would have a baby in their care, but she would never question it. Luz wasn't entitled to possess any information other than her cash.

CHAPTER 36

ONCE WIL HOPPED BACK on the interstate after Luke got more weaponry from Dan's old connect's house in Queens, Luke continued to torture Toby. His face was a bloody mess. Luke punched Toby with his hands covered with leather gloves. Wil never said a word. Toby tasted his own blood. His eyes were swollen, and Toby's nose was broken. Luke used a sharp pocketknife to slice flesh. Despite Toby's size, his pain tolerance was low. The pain started to become unbearable.

Toby panted. "Come on man, I'm just a worker! I was getting paid to watch you! Y'all got the address so what the fuck?"

Luke looked at a beaten, battered large mass of a man, and thought about some diabolical shit. Luke searched inside the bag of goodies he just got from Dan's boy, and pulled out a hand-sized drill. Luke outlined Toby's crotch with it.

"Luke, this ain't you man! Please! Don't do this!"

Toby's cell phone halted Luke's plan, but it was appreciated. Ike was calling.

"Get composed nigga. You better find out how many motherfuckers are at the barn, otherwise, I'm drilling a hole in your manhood," Luke said evenly.

On cue, Wil pulled over and put on the hazard lights. Toby took a deep breath before answering the phone on the fifth ring.

"Yeah boss."

"Update."

"Just left a capo robbery. This little nigga ain't playing."

"Love his sense of urgency. Good work Toby, but head back here at once. I need you at the farm for Orlando's drop off in the morning. Agustin is filling in for you, and you'll be the fourth man here guarding the Laws and product. He will head up there when you arrive. If Luke fails, it would be easier for Agustin to kill him. Robbie replaced Desmond."

"Why boss?"

"Desmond tried to rape Mr. Law's new love interest. I have no tolerance for that kind of fuckery. Any who, water under the bridge. Good work once again." Ike hung up. Toby couldn't believe Ike praised him, but it was no use. Luke's eyes were red and glossy. His nostrils flared. His left hand shook. Luke was about to lose it.

"You motherfucker!" Luke punched him repeatedly, and to the point where Wil had to intervene.

"Don't waste your energy on this fat son of a bitch. Preserve it for the real enemy." Luke punched Toby one last time before taking heed to Wil's advice.

Wil wheeled the black Escalade on dirt roads through a five-mile radius in New Jersey. The destination was getting closer. Toby remained bound and scared to death of Luke's unpredictable onslaughts, but Luke remained cool and collected. He was ready to cut down any one of Ike's men that came across his line of vision. Wil was ready as well, and planned to see another day.

Wil slowed the truck to a crawl. The farm was at least three acres. Livestock, cornfields, and farm machinery covered the land. Luke zeroed in on the barn. His family was in there. Luke became anxious, but he maintained it. Wil stopped the vehicle. Luke and Wil stepped out into the pitch-black morning that promised freezing rain, and met at the back of the truck. After Wil opened the rear end of it, Toby lookcd helpless, bloody, and exhausted, but he had enough energy to use his mouth.

"What's Agustin's number"

NEXT OF KIN

Toby ran the number off with no hesitation. Luke placed the cell phone next to Toby's mouth before he spoke.

...

Agustin paced the top level of the barn and waited for the go ahead from Ike. Leo, one of Ike's men, sat quietly and watched Agustin pace. Agustin been out of the assassin game for five years, but Ike's offer of twenty grand yanked him out of retirement. Connecticut was only three hours from where Agustin stood, and he'd be damned if he wasted the opportunity to collect easy money. The Argentinian traveled the world to complete contracts. Agustin knew American soil as well as his homeland. He'd been a Grim Reaper for men, women, and children. Agustin had no life, personality, or family. He killed for mega money, and he banked a lot of cash fucking with Ike.

Agustin stopped pacing, and he picked up Luke Law's picture on top of his profile. He was looking at a soon-to-be dead man. Agustin put the profile back on the tool table, and he rubbed the stubble on his face. Agustin knew what kind of man Ike was, and the death games Ike played, but he wasn't afraid of Ike and vice versa. There was an unspoken level of respect between the men. Agustin had no idea why he wanted Luke dead, and he didn't give a shit. Blood money was long and thick, and Agustin wanted it.

A stud in women's eyes, Agustin was a shade over six feet, and he was always suited and clean except for tonight. Agustin was dressed in a black sweat suit. His curly hair was always tied into a ponytail, and his hooded blue eyes pierced his victim's eyes and soul before he inflicted murder. Agustin made sure that his set of eyes would be the last ones victims saw before they met their maker.

Agustin stopped his pace when his phone vibrated. He looked on the screen; it was an incoming call from Toby. He cursed because he thought it was Ike.

"Yeah?"

"I'll be there in five minutes." Toby disconnected the call.

Agustin became suspicious. Toby wasn't due for hours. Agustin tried calling Ike on two lines, but they both went straight to voicemail, which was typical of him. Agustin locked, loaded, and carried precaution. He beckoned Leo to join him.

The henchmen descended down the stairs. Renee and Zora were still in captivity while the frail guard known as Spider watched them. Agustin stepped over the body Ike cut down an hour ago like it was part of the ground, and approached Spider.

"You speak to Toby?"

"No, why?" Spider asked.

Robbie, a slim, averaged sized man with beady eyes, walked in the entrance of the barn, and was the dead guard's replacement.

"Why the fuck is Toby sitting in the truck? That ugly four pie eatin' motherfucker scared to get wet?" Robbie asked candidly. Everyone laughed except the women and Agustin. Agustin smelled a set up.

"How do you know its Toby sitting in the truck? The windows are tinted, and too black for anyone to see inside. Robbie, Leo, come with me and keep your guns in your hands. Spider, you stay here with the women. Time spent away from them means more time for them to think," Agustin instructed.

When the men departed, Spider continued his tight watch on the women.

The rain spilled from the sky in an infernal downpour. Toby's black Escalade was being drenched, and visibility was shot. The men, led by Agustin, walked cautiously with their guns. Agustin walked slowly to the driver's window, and Robbie and Leo walked behind the truck. When Agustin opened the driver's side door, Toby wasn't in the driver's seat, but Agustin heard Toby's moans from the trunk of the truck.

Luke remained underneath the truck ready to make a move. The assassin's feet were two inches away from Luke's weaponry. With a long blade in one hand, and his gun in the other, Luke drew first blood by taking a slice at Agustin's left ankle. The pain forced Agustin to scream in agony, and fall to the muddy ground. In an instant, Luke and Agustin locked eyes. Luke inflicted a close range headshot, splattering Agustin's brain. The men who took the rear of the truck tried to react, but the two cronies didn't see Wil in the distance, and were caught in Wil's crosshairs. Robbie and Leo were savagely gunned down. Luke slid from underneath the truck, made sure the killers didn't have a pulse, and joined Wil as they made their way to the barn.

Spider heard gunshots, and he left the women. He walked towards the barn's entrance holding a semi-automatic rifle. Spider opened the barn door, and saw his cut down co-workers. The second Spider froze, Luke already had the gun pointed at Spider's back.

"Drop the weapon," Luke said sternly with Wil at his side.

Spider did just that.

"You don't have to take this far bro. I'll show you where they at," Spider said.

"You goddamn right. Walk," Luke said through clenched teeth. Spider walked them to a small room where the women were held. Renee and Zora's eyes lit up with relief and surprise at their men's appearance. Before Luke and Wil embraced the women, Luke shoved Spider harshly against the wall.

Luke said, "I'll never leave a stone unturned."

"Come on man, I showed you where..."

Luke and Wil opened fire on Spider in mid-sentence. Spider twisted, turned, and twitched before collapsing to the dirt ground. Renee and Zora were in shock.

"Y'all alright?" Wil asked while Luke cut the women loose.

"Luke, Ike has Baron! We have to go and get him!" Renee said frantically.

"I know Ma, but is there anyone else in this barn?"

"I don't think so," Renee said.

"We need to get the fuck out of here before more of Ike's men show up. Once we check y'all into a hotel, we go look for Baron. We have to hurry up!" Wil interjected.

Zora heard everything Wil said, but she was lost in Luke's embrace. Zora couldn't believe she was rescued. Luke let her go, gathered the cash the cronies were supposed to use for the cocaine drop, and escorted everyone out of the barn unscathed.

CHAPTER 37

Parsippany, New Jersey

LUKE AND WIL WERE tight-lipped and silent as they prepared weaponry in the truck while Toby remained bounded, but Toby provided them information of the camera's location of the mansion. The weather became significantly worse with rain and gusts of heavy wind, but it was on Luke and Wil's side. After Luke and Wil staked the mansion, the men knew they had enough tools to rescue Baron, but staying alive to use them was another thing. Death seemed highly likely for them, but Luke and Wil would try to avoid it at all costs. They weren't leaving New Jersey without Baron.

Wil shot out six covert and two network cameras. The power and lights in the mansion faded in and out because of the wind. If the guards in the swanky residence were hip, they would've spotted five dead Rottweiler. Thirty-five pounds of hamburger meat seasoned with cyanide exterminated them. Vomit and blood discolored the lawn from where they lay dead. It was inhumane, but the dogs weren't on Luke and Wil's side. They were flesh devouring assassins.

When the men holstered their last piece of weaponry, they exited the vehicle and walked around to the back of it. Luke lifted the rear door of the truck. Heavy wind and raindrops added a little relief to Toby's beaten and battered face. The glow from the lights flickered again in the mansion. Luke and Wil looked at Toby, and at one another. In silent agreement, they knew what had to be done. Luke beckoned Wil inside the truck.

NEXT OF KIN

"I...told you...everything..." A small geyser of blood spewed from Toby's mouth. "Don't do...this Luke...it is a mis..." Luke shoved the silencer down his throat, squeezed the trigger without giving it a second thought, and got inside the truck. Wil turned it on and drove through some of the property, parked in a space, exited it, and left it on the massive driveway in plain view, which was part of the plan.

Luz poured a small portion of *Henri Jayer* in Ike's glass as he sat in the dining room area drunk off his own success. Ike came a long way. His father would be proud. Ike accumulated enough wealth for him to support a generation, but he had no intention of walking away. Elizabeth was on her last leg; Ike felt it. Bruno lost his power years ago, but Elizabeth kept Bruno's allies. With Elizabeth dead, her allies and connects may disappear, and make Ike more vulnerable to enemies, and even some fake allies on the same team. Elizabeth was respected and deemed a don, but some of her allies wanted Ike dead because of his blatant disrespect towards the elite in the underworld. Ike came to a reality check; he needed to keep those allies intact. The reason why Ike still breathed was on the strength of his parents. With his stepmother dead, Ike was a sitting duck, and Ike knew he had to be political.

The muscle bound, curly haired Hispanic guard named Ricardo that overlooked security in the mansion walked into the dining room, and in front of Ike. Ike knew something was wrong with the guard being out of his station area. Ike looked at him incredulously.

"What seems to be the shortcoming? I'm not in the mood for any type of fuckery."

"I know, and I seriously hate to interrupt your moment, but is Toby still in Connecticut?"

"Not a concern of yours," Ike said curtly.

"I know," Ricardo said, shifting his eyes downward. He was petrified of Ike. The last guy that ran security got hit by a bullet, and fell to his death during working hours. The dude did it to himself by falling asleep, but the example Ike set was well received.

"So what is it man?" Ike asked thickly. "Speak!"

"I uh, thought Toby was trading off with Agustin at the farm. You spoke loudly sir, and you ordered me to keep the door open. I indirectly overheard your conversation a little while ago," Ricardo said nervously.

Ike finished off his drink. "What?"

Ricardo said, "Toby's truck is outside."

Ike contorted his face. Something wasn't clicking. Ike pulled out his cell phone, and dialed Agustin's number, but it rang repeatedly. He dialed it again, and got the same result. Ike dialed up one more of his contacts to check in on the farm before ending the call. Ike and the guard walked to the camera room. Ike looked at Toby's truck through the monitor, and noticed the rest of the monitors were black. Once Ike noticed, Ricardo cut him in.

"Our other problem, sir. The power has been off and on for the last three hours. When it comes back on, the rest of the monitors remain fuzzy and black. The cameras are securely mounted, and can withstand a biblical disaster. Someone destroyed the cameras."

Ricardo radioed another guard to watch the station. When the black suited, pale skinned, lazy eyed henchman walked into the door, Ike told him to stay put and watch the monitor. Ike and Ricardo loaded up with weapons, and headed out to investigate.

Ike and Ricardo walked slowly to Toby's truck with their rods on the ready. The rain was subsiding, but it was cold as shit. They moved cautiously around the truck, unable to see through the pitch-dark tints. Ike had the gun trained at the driver's side door, and used his other hand to open it. Ike inched it until the door was wide open. He looked through the interior, and spotted nothing unusual, but when Ricardo lifted the hatch, he gasped. Ricardo's eyes received an eyesore.

"Ike, someone is lurking around," Ricardo said.

Ike pulled himself from the driver's seat, and he joined his inferior at the rear of the truck. Ike looked at Toby's opened eye corpse with no emotion. The *Targus* bag holding Maximilian Coffman's head was in there as well. Questions circulated in Ike's mind, but he had no time to analyze and recall. Before Ike could utter a word, bullets whizzed by them and formed three holes on the truck's exterior. Instinctively, Ike and Ricardo took cover, and pointed their guns in all directions; they had no idea who or where the shooter was posted. Ricardo spotted someone running east, and fired shots at the intruder. Ricardo cut the imposter down with his last bullet. While the men caught their breath from the near death incident, they left their cover. Ike told Ricardo to check on the intruder he clipped. Ricardo made moves to the body. Ike and Ricardo went in the opposite direction.

Ike ran up the steps to his mansion, and knew the man Ricardo bucked wasn't alone. The front door was opened and he knew for certain he closed it behind him when they came outside to inspect. Ike knew he slipped badly. His stepmother was inside and resting comfortably. Ike bolted inside with her safety being the first priority. He radioed a guard, and stationed him to Elizabeth's room.

Vanessa looked at herself in the mirror, and knew she was dope. She ran a comb through her thick, wet mane. Her tanned Brazilian body was flawless, but she wondered why Ike treated her like a centipede that crawled from beneath a rock. Vanessa decoyed multiple assassinations for him; she would travel to the highest heat in hell if that were what Ike wanted to do. Tears trickled from her eyes thinking of the murder and torture Ike inflicted with her manicured hand in many of them. Vanessa helped him because she loved him. If Ike caught another murder case, he'd be pressing his luck, and would bring her down along with him.

Vanessa wrapped a towel around her body, and a scarf around her head. She planned on sucking Ike's limp dick until it was erect, and then hopping on it. She stopped taking her birth control without Ike's knowledge so she could trap him. Vanessa loved him, but without Ike, she'd be nothing. Losing her golden security blanket scared the shit out of her.

A soft knock took Vanessa out of her scandalous thoughts. She knew it was Ike. She opened the door without saying a word, and without discretion. The smile on Vanessa's face turned into a look of terror; she screamed for a second until she saw the barrel of Luke's gun. When Luke snatched her by her hair and held her against him, her towel fell to the floor. Luke inched his lips to her ear.

"Where's Ike, bitch?"

Vanessa was scared, but poised. She wasn't willing to be brave with a man coming for his own flesh and blood. She recognized Luke at first sight.

"He's here, but please don't kill me!" Vanessa pleaded.

Luke heard footsteps and thought fast.

"Vanessa, you all right?" the guard asked frantically as he barged into the bathroom, secretly hoping to catch her in the nude. He didn't see anyone in the massive bathroom, but the shower curtain made his curiosity peak. The guard yanked the dark red shower curtain and saw an empty, wet bathtub, but the guard stared at the emptiness a second too long before Luke crept out of the walk-in closet and shot him a few times with his silencer. The guard fell against the wall, and slid down it, making hardly any noise. After he snatched the bitch from up off the floor, he held her at gunpoint. Luke quietly escorted Vanessa out of the bathroom.

Three guards scrambled for their weapons in the hallway after Ike told them someone squeezed through security, and made it in the residence. Once the men equipped themselves, they moved hastily down the hallway, but their movement came to a crawl when Luke climbed up the last two steps of the plush, spiral staircase as he held Vanessa hostage.

"Put them guns down and your hands up before I pop this bitch," Luke said sternly. Luke held the gun tight enough on her temple to leave a mark.

"Come on man, think about what you're doing, and the shit you already did. Let her go bro," the leader of the three guards stated while they placed their weapons on the floor. One of the other guards had a set of balls. Luke caught it.

"Your finger even touch that steel, this bitch's brains will stain the walls. No funny shit."

The leader of the group beckoned them to full cooperation. The men complied.

Luke told them to turn around. The guards did so hesitantly. Luke removed the barrel away from her head, shoved Vanessa in front of him so she wouldn't pull any sneaky shit, and dumped the entire clip into the guards' heads and backs. Vanessa made a sudden move. She kicked Luke as hard as she could and made him fall. The gun fell from

Luke's hand and unto the floor. Vanessa tried to get away, but Luke grabbed her ankle, and she fell alongside him. Luke pulled the gun out of his ankle holster, positioned it on her flat stomach, and threatened to blow a ghastly hole through it.

Luke got up with his gun still positioned on her stomach, and told her to get up and walk. He needed her for leverage. Luke collected some of the fallen guard's weaponry, and limped further down the artistically decorated hallway. Luke's desire to bring home his son was so great that he felt no pain, caution, or fear.

When Ricardo turned Wil over to confirm his death, he was greeted with a piece of cold, jagged steel that Wil slid across his throat. Wil was never shot; he voluntarily dropped and stayed put until the guard was close enough for Wil to make his move. Having served in the marines, Wil was taught many survival tactics, and was trained to kill in physical combat. He was a peaceful man, but avoided trouble at all costs, and saved the deadly part of him for grave, unforeseen events. His girlfriend and her grandchild's kidnapping was an unforeseen event.

Wil made his way into the mansion. Since he was a retired detective, Wil still possessed the tools to access any home. He checked behind every door and looked to kill anyone that wasn't Luke or Baron. Wil never understood why Luke had an issue with him, but he loved Baron like the grandson he never had. Baron spent many nights at Renee's house, and he created a bond with the baby. Wil had no problem putting his life on the line for Baron.

Wil heard a small shuffling behind a closed door. He slowly turned the doorknob, and opened the door using caution. Wil sighed at the sight of the elderly woman laying in a hospital bed with rails on it. He had no room in his conscience to kill an innocent, but the woman had a mouth and a set of eyes. Wil placed a finger over his lips, and approached with the intent of smothering her with a pillow, but Elizabeth was ready for him. Without warning, she lifted the pump action tactical twelve-gauge and fired it. The impact of the shell knocked Wil hard against the wall.

Luke heard the shotgun blast and thud. He walked a nude Vanessa down two doors. Luke knew she would come in handy. Elizabeth heard someone lingering at the door, and she cocked her pump. Before Vanessa could beg for her life, Luke forcefully pushed Vanessa into the room, and into the line of the bullet. The bullet met her halfway, and it created more impact on her fall. The Brazilian beauty was dead before she hit the floor. Luke took cover with his weapon in hand. Luke sprang up quickly and busted a barrage of shots into Elizabeth's aging frame. Her body shook and thumped wildly within the short confines of her bed. The shells plugged in her made the smoke rise from her body.

Luke heard the faint sounds and grumbles from the guards as they made their approach to the door. Luke had no choice but to hide in the closet. The guards rushed in Helter Skelter, and found Elizabeth's body riddled with gunshots. The smoke was a sign of a fresh kill. One of them stepped over Wil, and got a closer look. Luke shifted in the large walk-in closet, and the guards heard it. With their semi-automatics, the guards released a volley of shots from them, lighting up the closet. Once they ceased fire, Luke shot through the closet door, clipped one guard in the pelvis, and shot the other one in his upper right chest. Luke wasn't hit, but the shelf in the closet was shot off, and it landed on his elbow. Wasting no time, Luke left the bullet-ridden closet, and added two more bullets to the slow crawling guards, making their death official. Luke tiptoed out of the room, but didn't get far.

Ike searched his entire home, and only found his dead staff. He sped- dialed a goon that was close to where the women were held, and found out everyone was dead, and the women were missing. Ike tried to avoid the idea that Luke actually had the balls to hold court in his home, but Toby's body lying curled up in his own truck, and Maximilian's head kept the probability high. Ike and Elizabeth had their fair share of enemies, and knew most of them, but why would his enemies find time to kill small fish? Toby was nothing more than a security guard who tracked and killed people for Ike's cash. Ike had a network of assassins; Toby was dispensable.

Ike's heartbeat sped up when he got closer to his stepmother's room. The door to her room was wide open, and the smell of death lingered. Paying attention to none of the bodies, Ike's mouth hung open at the sight of Elizabeth's shot up corpse. His hands trembled, and his legs were numb. Ike stepped over Vanessa's body, put his arms around his stepmother, and screamed out in agony. Reality set in, and

Ike snapped out of his grief. He picked his gun up off his stepmother's body, and trained it at the opened door, but Luke trained his weapon at him at the same time. Luke and Ike locked eyes, and stared down one another intensely. Several months ago, Luke was bound to a chair with fear seeping through his pores. Ike had derived pleasure from Luke's fear, but now there was a new scent emanating from Luke's skin. Ike now smelled a man soaked with vengeance.

"One of us isn't leaving this room alive I see. I misjudged you; you and your friend single-handedly destroyed my muscle, my dogs, my pride, and the woman that groomed me along with my father. You will die for that." Ike's tone was dry, grimy, and deadly. Luke smiled insanely at Ike, and Luke continued to point his heat at him. Luke looked Ike squarely in his eyes.

"Just like I'm not leaving here without my son."

Ike's eyes were flooded with tears with the tip of his finger resting on the trigger. He was thrown off by his stepmother's death, but Ike's aim remained accurate.

"I fed your son to my pets, you know, the ones you killed, since your mother and girlfriend disappeared. Go out there and carve him out yourself. One of them probably shat Baron," Ike said icily.

Tears of revenge and anger spilled down Luke's face. The anger he carried clouded him. Luke pulled the trigger first, but the gun was empty. Luke dropped the gun, and knew he was gonna get shot. Ike cracked a sinister smile, dropped his weaponry, and moved forward in Luke's direction. Luke braced himself for the fight of his life as he met Ike halfway. Refusing to be struck first, Luke threw a jab with his left, but Ike read and timed it. Ike blocked Luke's punch, and in that split second, Ike managed to go in his inside pocket, scoop a knife from it, and counter with a swipe. The cut was deep, and Luke grimaced and screamed with pain. Luke staggered back. Ike lunged forward, and sliced Luke across the arm. Luke yelled out even louder. Luke's chest and arm screamed with pain. Without thinking, Luke swung with the right hand, but was countered again with a blade that touched the skin of his stomach. Seeing no other option, Luke made a feeble attempt to charge him, but Ike pivoted and shoved him harshly against Elizabeth's dresser. Cosmetics, medication, and jewelry fell to the floor. Ike rushed at Luke and kicked him in the stomach, and Luke curled up. Ike caught a glance of Elizabeth, and her dead body gave him more fuel to punish

Luke. Ike stomped and kicked Luke, and in the midst of all that, Luke secured the small glass jar after secretly fishing for it in his pocket while he endured a beating. If Luke weren't cut, he would've gotten the foreign object a lot faster. Luke had a high threshold for pain, but his fresh wounds that Ike kicked and punched made the pain he had unbearable. Fighting Ike to the death would be useless.

Ike took a step back. "All you had to do was pay your brother's debt and you'd have your family back, and now I'm on a verge of killing you. I killed your son already. And I will track and kill the rest of your family." Ike moved forward and turned him over with his leg, but Luke grabbed his ankle, knocking Ike off balance momentarily, and it was all the time Luke needed. Ike was smart, skilled, and fast enough to dodge punches and kicks, but the sulfuric acid Luke flung at his face from the glass jar was faster. Ike recoiled in a hot fury of pain. The chemical went into both eyes, and it melted the orbitals and the side of his face. Ike screamed violently, and was more dangerous. He swung his knife recklessly in Luke's direction, but Luke moved. The pain in Luke's arm, chest, and stomach roared as he pulled out the gun he had in his ankle holster. Ike ran around the room, and swung his knife wildly. Luke made it to his feet and leaned on Elizabeth's bed, and tried to get a clean shot. Luke could see the skin drip from Ike's once handsome face, and the skeleton behind it. Ike moved so wildly around the room that Luke couldn't get a steady aim, but Wil helped him by tripping Ike. Ike fell onto Elizabeth's body. Luke quickly centered his gun at Ike and squeezed off. The bullets made Ike's body rattle with his stepmother's corpse. Blood, brain matter, and pieces of Elizabeth's body spewed everywhere. Luke grilled Ike and Elizabeth's body with no remorse.

Wil rose from the floor, and he quietly thanked God for his bulletproof vest, but the men knew the mission wasn't complete. After Luke placed one more bullet into Ike's remains, Luke and Wil left the room. Luke prayed that Ike was bluffing about his son being fed to the dogs.

Luke and Wil stepped over bodies, walked through bloody hallways, and killed a guard who was hanging onto life by a thread. The men stopped walking when they heard Baron's cries from a room they approached. Luke and Wil checked their ammunition before they entered the room. Wil walked in first. Wil's body language told Luke that Baron wasn't in there.

"He's alive though," Wil whispered as the men inspected the Fisher Price radio. Luke was getting antsy, and had an urge to smash the walkie-talkie.

After they backed out of the room, Baron's cries continued to flood the still, dead silence in the mansion. Luke and Wil split up. Luke walked upstairs to the second level and pointed his gun everywhere. When Baron cried again, Luke knew he was close. Luke tiptoed and had his gun at the ready before walking into the maid's room. Luz held Baron and gently rocked him. She sang a nursery song to Baron in Spanish. Luz knew someone was at the door, and took note of the presence.

"What do you want with baby?"

"He's my baby. Give 'em up before you get added to the death toll." Luke was hot, emotional, hurt, and unstable. If Baron wasn't in her arms, she'd be bleeding by now.

"Then I stay with baby."

Luz was firm and stubborn. She was gonna be a problem if Luke didn't think fast.

Luz said, "Or I could put baby down and we talk deal."

Luke contorted his face. His pain was getting worse, and didn't have time to reason with anyone.

"What the fuck is there to deal about?! Give me my son!" Luke yelled so loud that mucus came out of his mouth.

"If you want son, you corporate," Luz said nonchalantly.

 He decided to play her game.

"Let's talk." Releasing those two words were like pulling teeth. Luke's cuts bled badly, and he needed medical attention. Luz placed Baron back in the small crib. She tucked him in before Wil's bullet ended her plan. The bullet entered the back of her head, and came out through the front. Luz body slumped over the crib; thankfully, Baron wasn't hurt. Wil peeped the entire exchange outside the doorway when she had her back turned. Luz was reaching for the Glock 26 that shared the crib with Baron.

Luke ran to the crib and scooped him. Luke held his son closely to his chest while Wil covered him in case there were more guards. Luke and Wil looted some cold, hard cash off some of the bodies, and they collected jewelry from the rooms on their way out. Once outside the mansion, Wil managed to hot-wire a car and get it started. Luke and Wil climbed in the car, drove near the hotel they checked the women into, and hopped out of it, leaving the vehicle on the side of the road.

Cops and ambulances pulled up seconds after Luke, Wil, and Baron left the property. The news and media would plant theories about Ike and Elizabeth's adversaries that possibly lead to their demise, but they would never point a finger on a square like Luke.

The next day, after they got rid of every weapon they had, and getting cleaned and patched up, Luke, Zora, Wil, Renee, and Baron boarded a train back to Connecticut. It would be a painful ride for Luke, but his family was safe and intact; that was all that mattered.

EPILOGUE

One year later

AFTER BEING SENTENCED TO sixty-five years last week for the murder of Timmy Blairwood, Omar couldn't shake the deadly glare in Luke's eyes at his sentencing. There was no proof that Omar murdered Steve, but Renee and Luke knew he was guilty so they went to see him off for good. Omar avoided eye contact with the Laws throughout the proceedings. Renee used to feed and bathe Omar as a youth, and in return, he murdered her eldest child. When the judicial marshals escorted Omar out of the courtroom, Omar stole one last look at Luke. He would never forget the smirk Luke held on his face for the rest of his days.

Monroe, a thin, dreaded, thick bearded man from Hartford convicted of capital murder a few months ago, was sitting tight on his bunk with no display of emotion about shooting and killing a cop. He knew his life was over as soon as it began. Not too many people fucked with Monroe. He walked around in strong silence, but Monroe minded his business. A few cats that tried to get a name for themselves tested him, but they ended up in the infirmary.

When Omar started his sentence, Monroe took him under his wing. Getting life in prison wasn't a surprise to Monroe. He was a recidivist. Monroe couldn't function in society, and he had no problem running away from responsibilities. Monroe's life had been a lonely road for him, and he had nothing to miss on the outside besides his elderly mother. Monroe was a lifer. Omar looked forward to talking with Monroe; he eased some of the tension in his head. Omar would be an old man before he'd be considered for parole. Monroe kept it real with him though. He'd tell Omar that he was never going home again, or more than likely would never fuck or taste pussy. Omar couldn't help but smirk because he knew Monroe was right, but the thought of him never finding true love, and being locked up with men for the rest of his life made him nauseous.

"I think given a choice, I'd take the chair over this life shit. What kind of life do I have in here?" Omar asked.

The high profile offender wondered the same thing.

"The kind of life we deserve. We all make choices; we just made the bad ones, you know what I mean? But in the meantime, you can be free if you put your mind to it," Monroe said encouragingly.

Omar laughed. "How the fuck is *that* gonna happen? God? Allah?"

Omar laughed again at the thought of Allah or God walking him to his freedom. Omar and Monroe were close, but Omar was never fond of religion, and he held many disbeliefs. Monroe would bury that shit on someone until he made them believers.

"Me," Monroe said grimly. He pulled out a shank made from a Poland Spring bottle. Omar stared at the weapon, and at Monroe holding it with a face that bore no expression. Omar got nervous, but he concealed his anxiety.

"Damn bro, you kinda marking me. Quit playing."

"You've been marked since the first day you got here." Monroe's facial expression didn't change.

Omar took a deep breath, and had a sense of what was going on.

"Yo, what's good man?"

In an instant, Monroe grabbed him by his neck, and Monroe pinned him on the floor. Monroe was thin, but his strength wasn't. Omar called for the C/O, but his cries weren't heard. Monroe placed his lips next to Omar's ear.

"Luke and Q send their condolences. This is for my little brother Blake!" Monroe gutted Omar until he stopped moving. Monroe stabbed Omar thirty times after his soul left his body. Omar's face and head looked like raw hamburger meat loaded with blood. Monroe heard the faint correctional officers footsteps coming from a distance. Monroe kneeled over the body, and he put his hands in the air. Monroe knew he was on his way to Northern, but it was in the name of his brother Blake, whose door Steven and Timmy knocked on but got no answer. Blake was cut down an hour before Steven. Blake was all set to have his hand in the biggest city drug take-over in Waterbury, Connecticut history. That was Monroe's opportunity to shine, but Omar threw a deadly wrench in their plans. Monroe felt the system gave him a license to kill by giving him life without parole. The only difficulty Monroe had in the task was befriending Omar, but it was worth it. Monroe's charge and conviction made Quincy a true believer in fate. Luke and Quincy didn't have to shed a dime.

Pandemonium and chaos roared through the prison when code blue was announced. The correctional officers, one of them held a miniature camcorder, extracted Monroe out of his cell. The cell extraction wasn't necessary, but the C/Os were highly trained and knew the inmate could have been looking for a chink in their armor. Monroe went down peacefully and felt good about avenging his brother and Steven's murder.

Luke walked around the house and held a cell phone to his ear. He got an ear full of Talisha's bullshit. She copped a plea, and she only did a year and two months. Talisha neared the release of her time in a halfway house in Maryland, and she thought she was gonna come out and jump back in the mix of things, but Luke had other plans, and a commitment to Zora.

"Its like that Luke? You are going to just throw me out of your life?" Talisha asked incredulously.

Luke paused in his travels on his final walkthrough to see that they weren't leaving anything behind.

"That's exactly how it is. What the fuck do you want from me? I paid for your freedom, and I took those bullshit anger management classes thanks to you calling the cops on me. I think you can take over from there."

"Fuck you Luke! I want to be a mother to my son!" Luke could hear Talisha crying.

"So its fuck me, huh? You weren't thinking about being a mother when you let niggas take your pussy, or criticizing me when I took care of your funky ass. And you stole my safe."

Talisha kept quiet on that one.

"Look, I'm a man, and I would never deprive you of being Baron's mother, but you are going to have to do it from a distance. I don't love you Talisha, and you shouldn't blame me. You need to move on."

"I see you moved on with that bitch Zora."

Luke smirked.

"That bitch is my fiancée, and she is carrying my seed."

The phone went silent. It was only for a few seconds, but it seemed like an hour.

"Really Luke? Then you know what, I will fight to get him back. You ain't lettin' that bitch raise my son!" Talisha yelled.

"She is more like a mother to him then you'll ever be. I don't need to nag her to change diapers, or not to smoke weed while he's sleeping in the crib. She doesn't leave him alone in the crib crying when you and your slut crew be in the next room smoking trees. She works! She goes to school! She encourages me and never belittles me. You disrespected me for years; that shit would never happen again. So go ahead, try to take him. You have no job, money, or life. You're just the womb Baron came out of. Luckily, Zora was there to pick up where you never left off!"

Talisha hung up.

Luke pocketed his phone, and continued to journey around Renee's house one last time before the family was due to hit the road. Once Luke inspected the house, something told Luke to check the attic. Luke was sure he and Wil moved everything out of it, but his conscience wouldn't let him walk away without checking. Luke walked to the attic door, pulled the string, unfolded the ladder, and walked up there. His eyes scanned the area and spotted nothing. On Luke's way down the steps of the ladder, his foot slipped from the first rung. Luke gripped the floor of the attic to prevent himself from falling through the ceiling. As his fingers clawed the surface of the maple wood, one of the floorboards loosened beneath Luke's hold. His feet gained their bearings, and he propelled himself back up the ladder to investigate the loose plank of wood. When Luke lifted the floorboard, his heart leapt in his chest when he saw a large tote covered with years of dust. Luke pulled the bag from the cloud of thick dust. He didn't know how he and Wil missed it. Luke pulled the bag to the middle of the floor. Upon further inspection, the zipper had a lock on it. Luke removed his folding knife from his pocket, and he cut the bag open. Hundred dollar bills spilled out of it. Luke's mouth was wide open. The large tote bag was filled with hundreds up to the brim. Luke stuffed the money back into the bag, looked around one last time, and climbed down the steps of the attic. Once Luke folded the ladder and put the door that held the ladder back in place, Renee walked in with Baron followed by Zora and Wil.

"Luke, we need to get out..."

Renee's speech was cut short when a hundred dollar bill floated unto the floor. Zora held her large stomach, looking as shocked as Wil.

"Where did you find that?" Renee asked.

Luke said, "In the attic! When I went to see Quincy, he told me Steve had a stash somewhere hidden, and I just found it. Half of it goes to Quincy though; he deserves that respect."

No one argued that. Quincy's information made Luke victorious when his family was kidnapped. Luke paid his dues. He had the money that he never gave to Ike, which was now way more than Ike demanded. The Laws rode high, despite their anguish of dealing with their horrific past. After Luke placed the money in another bag, Renee and Wil took Baron out the house, leaving Zora behind.

"I wish my mom could come with us," Zora said sadly.

"I know, but she'll come around when she comes for the first visit. One day in our new place in Santa Monica will change anyone's mind," Luke said kindly. Luke loved Zora's mother like his own. "You need to use the bathroom?"

"I just did baby," Zora said, planting a soft, wet kiss on his lips. She hugged Luke afterwards.

Zora said, "I love you so much."

"I love you too," Luke replied, hugging her even tighter. After they broke the embrace, Zora joined Renee in the car. Wil was in the driver's seat of the U-Haul waiting for Luke.

Luke washed his hands and face. He shut the water off, and took a good look at himself in the mirror. He removed his shirt where the reminder of Ike's knife remained. The scars healed, but Luke's head was on fire. He made many bodies drop in order to get his family back, and Luke almost lost his life on several occasions. Luke looked at Ike's grotesque face after he dumped the acid on him every time he closed his eyes. Luke would rise from his sleep abruptly. If Ike's ghost didn't haunt him at night, the guilt Luke felt associated with Dan's death substituted it, but neither nightmare held more weight than the other. Despite the mental anguish of it, Luke would do it all over if his family were taken from him again.

After walking out the bathroom, and out of the house Luke was raised in, he looked back at it again. Luke's cell phone killed his moment, but he smiled at the caller.

"Hello," Luke chirped into the phone.

"Hi, Luke?"

"This is he. May I help you?"

"This is Diane, your program director. Guess what? The investigation is over! The consumer accused of killing John is officially out of the program. When can you start?"

"Hope everything is well Diane, but I've moved on, but thank you anyway," Luke said politely. He tried to hurry Diane off the phone.

"Luke, please, I can't lose anymore staff, especially you. Is there anyway that I can talk you into staying?"

"Not at all. I'm happy," Luke said.

"Can you sleep on it and call me in the morning? I think we can give you a fifty cent raise for your troubles."

Luke placed his hand on the receiver and chuckled.

"I don't think that would be necessary, but thanks and good luck to you," Luke said before he ended the call. Luke walked to the truck and climbed in.

"Motherfuckers is offering me my job back," Luke said incredulously.

"After a year and accusing y'all of murder? Fuckin' people got a lot of nerve," Wil said.

"And she offered me a fifty cent raise for my troubles." Luke and Wil laughed in unison. They knew they would never have to work a day in their lives again. Luke and Wil made some investments with

NEXT OF KIN

some of the money, and it tripled. Santa Monica was the ideal location for getting away from the horrid memories, and chilling out through the second phase of their lives around blue water and white sand.

Wil gunned the engine and drove quietly down the street with Renee, Zora, and Baron behind them. It would take them four days to get there. Instead of looking back, Luke and his family looked forward to the endless possibilities that existed for them out in California.

Made in the USA
Middletown, DE
26 October 2020